THE LONE WOLF

Yulia Sonbergh

CONTENTS

1, IN THE HOLE

"**I**'m going to ask you one more time."

Fox startled out of his stupor. He had been half-dozing again, remembering a dark time, similar to this one, maybe worse, maybe the same, depending on how this all went down. He refrained from looking directly at the small group in the room with him. He glanced at their feet, the only sign of acknowledgment he'd give them.

All of them were Alphas. Two women and two men. He was having a hard enough time with all of them being in the same room and all of their attention on him, he could hardly look at them, let alone speak to them.

"What is your name?" One of the male Alphas asked. He had asked it five times already, over the course of the evening, or the day, or the night. There were no windows down here, in this dark cement hole. He had no idea what time it was, or how much time had passed. He just knew that he was hungry, and thirsty. The only light right now came from a single lantern they had set on the floor.

Fox remained silent, fear and exhaustion keeping his mouth shut. He could hardly muster a strained mumble, or even a hum.

The Alphas waited for a moment, and once it became apparent that Fox wasn't going to answer, the male Alpha threw his hands up and turned to the staircase leading up out of the hole. "I'm over this. He can stay and rot down here for all I care."

The remark didn't sting Fox; he had heard worse and had been expecting that kind of reaction anyway. The other male Alpha sighed heavily and followed after the first Alpha. After a moment, one of the women left, too. Only one Alpha remained.

She stood there for a long while, quiet, probably thinking, staring at Fox where he sat on the floor of his cell, knees tucked up and arms wrapped loosely around his shins, his forehead resting against his knees.

Eventually, the Alpha crouched down, resting on the balls of her feet, elbows propped on her thighs. "If you answer my questions, I'll let you pick between three choices of something fresh for your dinner tonight." Ah, so it was evening, or at least late afternoon. Fox felt a small rush of relief at knowing what it might look like outside. "And if you still refuse to talk, then all you will get is leftover scraps from someone else. Do we have a deal?"

It wasn't much of a deal, rather than coercion. Fox was undeniably hungry, though, and he didn't want half-eaten scraps. Something warm and filling sounded a thousand times better.

It took some inner encouragement and some strength to muster up enough of his voice to speak. But he managed. "With... water... too?"

He couldn't see it, but he could feel her smiling in triumph. "Yes," she said. "With water, too."

"Fox," he told her.

"What?" she asked, predictably confused. Fox licked his lips and tried to clear his throat.

"My name... It's Fox," he whispered.

"Oh," the woman replied. "That's an interesting name. Don't think I've heard of a werewolf named Fox."

Fox wanted to say that he named himself, but he didn't have the energy for unnecessary chit chat.

"So, Fox. What made you want to trespass in our territory?" she asked. Fox thought it was a funny way of wording that question. What made him want to? It had been an accident. Their territory was so huge they needed four Alphas to run everything smoothly. He thought he'd been traversing through yet another town on his hitchhiking journey. He was a passenger in a car of a kind old man willing to help someone out, and the moment Fox felt the shift of a strong territory line passing underneath him, he immediately demanded to stop the car and for the old man to let him out. The man obliged, although confused, and Fox attempted to run right back the way they had come, but it was already too late. A pack wolf spotted him, pointed him out, made a big commotion about seeing Fox in the territory, and soon he was being tackled to the ground and pinned there. A group of Betas had tied his wrists and ankles and gagged his mouth, and then he was dragged to this small little hole in the ground, locked behind bars. Not long later, the Alphas showed up for interrogation.

It was all a big misunderstanding. Fox wished he could make them see that, but he knew they wouldn't. Every pack he'd encountered had proved that much to him. Every werewolf in the world either hated or feared lone wolves. They were unnatural, unpredictable, and often carried dangerous baggage.

"Didn't want to... I was hitchhiking. The man driving drove into your town, and I tried-" Fox's voice caught and he had to cough. "Tried to run back out."

"Sure," the woman replied. "A likely story. You wandered in by accident. Do you have any idea how many times I've heard that? Every lone wolf has wanted something from us. How am I supposed to believe you're any different?"

Fox should've known that she wouldn't believe him. Nobody ever believed him when he tried to make his case. He sighed in such a way that both his gut and shoulders sagged immensely, a full body shift, a complete internal decision to give up.

The Alpha went quiet again. Thinking, again. "Was it the food?" she asked eventually. Fox wondered what their food situation was like. For such a big pack they surely had to have a solid system in place, an abundance of sorts, ensuring that no one was left wanting. Abundance meant plenty to go around, and plenty enough left over for someone to steal. It made sense. A logical reason to trespass.

But Fox shook his head.

"Our Omegas, then? Looking to score a mate or a victim for trafficking?" she suggested next. Also a likely reason. Omegas were small and didn't have a lot of upper body strength, so snatching them was easy, and a common problem among many packs in the werewolf community. A lot of werewolves, Fox had learned, had a really intense breeding kink.

Fox shook his head again. He wasn't interested in Omegas.

"Attempting to settle a score with someone you met in the past?" she tried. Fox had met many people, most of whom had wronged him in some way. He had ached for revenge at some points, but realized it was futile and would only serve to hurt him more. He would rather forget he ever met any of them than try and go back to hurt them.

He shook his head.

"Medical supplies? Survival supplies? You must be here for something," she responded. Fox could hear in her voice that she was starting to get frustrated. He didn't want to lose his chance to eat a good meal, so he steeled his nerves as best he could and turned his head to meet her eye.

She was buff like most female Alphas, all corded muscle and scarred skin from proving herself to adversaries. Her dark brown hair was cut in a short bob, jaw length and tucked behind her ears. Her eyes were also brown, and they were full of attentiveness and intelligence.

"I am trying to head West," he croaked, "I was hitchhiking. I trespassed by accident."

He tried his best to hold her gaze, which on its own was a heavy thing to compete with. She seemed like she was trying to dig the answer out of his brain by just looking at him. She still didn't believe him, of course.

"You've heard of Lily of the Valley Pack, haven't you?" she asked him.

Fox had. They were known for being one of the highest functioning packs out there, one of the largest, and one of the packs with the best of the best. Good housing, good schooling, good food. Good fighters, good hunters, good Omegas. Strong-as-a-rock Alphas and loyal-to-the-end Betas. It was a common destination for many were-wolf families who'd been dislodged from their own packs, even if the process to get accepted was lengthy and not guaranteed. Fox figured that if there was ever an apocalypse, this pack would keep living each day as if nothing had happened, because they were so self-sustainable.

He didn't realize this was Lily of the Valley Pack. He didn't know if he should consider himself lucky, or so unlucky he might as well send his last prayers to the stars and wait for them to bury him six feet under.

Lily of the Valley Pack never, ever released the wolves who trespassed in their land. The lone wolves were never integrated or accepted, they were thoroughly hated, humiliated, and imprisoned for the rest of their lives, serving the pack however the pack deemed fit.

Fox held in a low whine of defeat and turned his head away. He closed his eyes and rested his head against his knees again. "I'm not getting any warm food, am I?" he asked quietly.

"I didn't say that. Technically you complied and answered my questions. I'm going to reconvene with the other Alphas to see if you're really lying or not. But you'll get your food and water," she said. Surprise briefly elated Fox, a swell in his chest, a trickle of hope.

"Spaghetti, steak, or chicken stew?" she asked. Fox's mouth watered at just the thought of those foods.

"S-st-steak, please. Thank you," he stammered, his mind reeling for a moment.

The Alpha stood, picking up the lantern, and without another word, she left. Fox heard the clang of a metal door slamming shut at the top of the stairs. Fox was left alone in darkness once more, but he didn't feel its claustrophobic dread. He gratefully awaited his food.

The Alpha came back some indeterminable amount of time later. She carried the lantern and a tray with her, and Fox immediately sat up straight as the smell of cooked meat filled his nose. The Alpha paused in front of his cell door, and jerked her chin up in a "move" motion. "Scoot back. To the wall."

Fox did as she said, backing up and crouching by the far wall, as far from her as he could get. The Alpha set the lantern on the floor, then pulled out a big iron key and unlocked the cell door. She narrowed her eyes at him, daring him to try attacking her as she stepped in, but

Fox only had eyes for the tray of food in her hands. He swallowed down the buildup of saliva in his mouth.

She set the tray down, then backed out and locked the door. Once he heard the click of the mechanism, he dove for the food. He grabbed the steak with his fingers and took one big bite. The meat was warm and savory, spices and seasoning erupting on his tongue. He chewed, and tasty juice spilled out from the meat. Fox groaned in delight, closing his eyes.

The Alpha watched as he ate. Fox knew it was better to space out his eating so he could enjoy the warm meal for longer, and so he wouldn't upset his stomach. He chewed each bite thoroughly, and chased each swallow with a swig of cool, crisp, clean water. His plate also had a serving of green beans and mashed potatoes, which he ate between every few bites of steak. He scraped his plate clean of any leftovers, and downed his glass of water to the very last drop he could get.

When he was done, he glanced up at the Alpha's knees. "Thank you very much," he told her, genuine but still quiet.

"You're welcome," she replied, neither warmly nor coldly. "So. The other Alphas and I have decided that it doesn't matter whether or not you're in our territory by accident. You're staying." Fox's shoulders grew tense and he curled his fingers over his thighs. "You've been fairly docile so far, so we've decided to make you our personal servant.

You're going to do exactly what we say, when we tell you to do it, and you're not going to put up a fuss about it. If you do, we'll be quick to show you what little tolerance we have for complaining or back-talking. Any acts of aggression will be met with punishment, and if you continue to be aggressive, we're going to move you to a much less pleasant position of servitude. Am I clear?"

Fox had been through worse. He'd spent two weeks in cells like this in other packs before. He'd been chased down or chased away. He'd been hunted like he was a rabid animal before. He had been captured on multiple occasions. He had been beaten up, tortured, neglected, starved. He had even been experimented on by a group of scientists, arguably the darkest time in Fox's life that he could remember, and he tried his best not to remember it at all. He had made friends and lost friends, he had been betrayed, screwed over, stepped on, and even arrested a few times. He had watched death, caused death, and narrowly escaped death. Being a servant to some Alphas was not the worst thing Fox could be forced into. And so, he didn't protest.

"Okay..." was all he said in reply. The Alpha frowned a little, probably not expecting such immediate submission from a lone wolf. Fox was sure that the other lone wolves they had imprisoned had put up at least some sort of fight. Fox had very little fight left in him, and he tried to reserve it for when it mattered most.

"Good. Come on, then," she said, and unlocked the door again. Fox rose from his spot on the floor, his muscles aching. He took a moment to stretch a little.

"I'm Alpha Leyra," she greeted, picking up the lantern. Fox picked up his food tray. She led him up a steep set of stairs and out of the hole. Fox had to squint his eyes at the sudden brightness of daylight. He blinked, blinked, blinked some more, and finally his eyes adjusted.

It was overcast outside, dark gray and navy blue thunderclouds promising rain soon to come. He was in the middle of a small field, the entrance to the hole a mere square door in the ground. Tall and well-grown oak trees surrounded the field, and knee-high wild grass grew around their trunks and roots. Fox took a deep breath of fresh air, glad to be out of the dark cell.

"Come on. We'll show you how your new life is going to go from now on," Leyra said, and Fox followed her as she led him to a small break in the trees.

~

2, A Place to Stay

The path through the woods was a longer one than Fox had been expecting, and he realized it was a different path than the one the Betas had dragged him down. He followed Leyra in silence, keeping an arm's length distance. He took advantage of his position behind her and studied her physique a little more.

Leyra had broad, strong shoulders, thick muscled thighs and upper arms, and Fox deduced that she would have no problem lifting him up above her head and chucking him twenty feet away. He noticed that she had a light brown skin color, and a tattoo of a starling on her forearm. She was also taller than him by at least four inches, maybe. Fox felt small next to her, even though on his own, "small" wouldn't be a word most would describe him as.

Leyra looked back at him, probably feeling his gaze. He averted his eyes downward, watching his feet as he walked. "So how much baggage can we expect from you?" she asked. Her tone suggested that she had asked that question many times before. Fox wondered just how many lone wolves had trespassed here.

"How much do you think I have?" Fox asked, curious about what she thought of him by just appearance alone. He tried to keep his tone light and polite. He didn't want to get on anyone's bad side right off the bat. Or at least, not more so than he already was.

He glanced up at her face to gauge her reaction to his question, and saw her eyes were narrowed and her lips were pressed in a thin line. Fox couldn't tell if she was thinking, or mildly affronted. Fox lowered his gaze again.

"You seem like you carry a lot of grief," she said. Fox's heart squeezed in his chest. He wondered if it was the slouch in his shoulders, or the downward tilt of his chin, or maybe his not-so-confident gate. Maybe it was in his eyes, a certain emptiness she could see. Sometimes grief was easy to spot, if it came in the form of apathy, sadness, or anger. Fox didn't care about hiding any of that. Well, he didn't have much energy for anger anymore.

"Am I right?" she pressed. She didn't sound haughty, but she didn't sound completely sympathetic, either. Maybe a lot of the lone wolves here carried grief, and there was only so much sympathy to go around. She probably had to keep her head in the Alpha game.

"Yes..." Fox murmured.

"Who did you lose?" Leyra asked. Fox thought that these questions were too personal for having just met. He didn't think he owed her an answer until they knew each other better; until Fox knew whether or not she cared at all. He kept silent.

Alpha Leyra waited for a few moments, then relented. "Not ready to say? That's fine," she said. "Just don't let your grief become a problem."

Fox felt a sting of indignation in his gut. So they thought that grief was a problem? Something no one else should deal with? He wondered what tragedy the pack members could've possibly gone through, if any at all. There probably wasn't a lot of death here, none that mattered. Fox had a feeling that no pack wolf here understood just how much it hurt to lose someone you loved. They probably didn't understand other forms of grief that Fox had experienced, either. Losing a friend to a stranger, losing a companion to a different path, losing belongings that you worked hard to get. All of those amounted to emotional loss, especially when you were a lone wolf.

"Have you lost anyone?" Fox asked, voice vaguely heated with hurt. He stared at her head, and she glanced back at him again.

"No. And, sorry. I'm not discrediting your loss, but I need you to understand it's important not to let your grief cause you to harm others. You hurt someone here, there's not a lot of forgiveness for you. It doesn't matter if you hurt someone because you're hurting. You need to figure out a healthy way to let out that pain," she told him.

Fox had a feeling that this pack didn't provide healthy outlets, and he was expected to figure it out on his own. He closed his eyes and took a deep breath, brushing away his annoyance and offense. It didn't matter. He wasn't planning on getting into any fights, regardless of how badly his grief was hurting him at times. He had already learned that it was better to let his grief out when he was alone, and not in the company of others.

"Anything else I should know about? Any triggers?" Leyra asked next. Fox mentally flipped through the pages of his memories for anything that had really affected him badly. Abandonment was one, but he had learned to expect that, so it wasn't really a trigger. Betrayal was another thing he already expected. He thought about all the times he'd gotten angry or upset. He thought about all the times he'd been terrified and in pain.

"I... I don't like the smell of antiseptic, or latex. I don't like hospitals, or doctors," he admitted.

"Hmm. Duly noted. I'll make sure you're kept away from the medical sector," she said. A minor feeling of emotional whiplash came over

Fox. How could she have no sympathy for expressing hurt through violence, but have enough to promise him he'd be kept away from things he was afraid of?

Maybe it was just another way for her to ensure he wouldn't panic and hurt someone. Maybe there was no sympathy involved at all.

Fox was starting to feel unsure about how well he would fare here. He reminded himself that he already knew 99% of people he met didn't care about him or his feelings.

After a good while of walking, they finally made it to the edge of the woods. The path opened up to another grass field, but a much larger one. Fox took in the sight of four distinctly large houses, spaced out along one big dirt path. That dirt road led down a small hill and wound around through more trees. As Fox followed it with his eyes, he spotted more buildings farther away in the distance.

Rain landed on his cheek, then his arm. He looked at the ground and noticed that it was starting to sprinkle, wet spots dotted sparsely along the soil around him. He turned his gaze to the sky, and noticed the clouds had significantly darkened during their walk.

"Let's get inside before it starts pouring," Leyra said. Fox followed her as she led him across the field to one of the houses. The house she took him to was brown with green trim, with lots of windows varying in size and shape. They took a few steps up to a wooden porch, where Fox noticed a few hanging pots where String-of-Pearls grew. Leyra unlocked the front door and stepped inside. A strong smell of eucalyptus wafted over Fox, and the smell staved off any anxiety he felt towards entering the house.

He stepped in. He noticed Leyra toe off her shoes, and did the same. He placed them in a partially hidden spot behind a small bench in the entryway, so no one would find his shoes easily and take them.

"Leyra? That you?" another woman's voice called from deeper in the house.

"Yes. I have a lone wolf with me, too," Leyra responded. She set the lantern down on the small bench, then gestured to Fox. "We can leave that tray in the kitchen," she said.

Fox followed her through the house. Dark hardwood floors were cool on his feet, and simple but boho-chic decorations filled empty spaces on the walls. Their furniture looked simple as well, but comfortable. As they entered the kitchen, Fox laid eyes on the other woman he'd heard.

In height, she reached up to Leyra's chin, and she had dark skin and dark eyes, and her coiled hair was done up in two small buns atop her head. She wore a flower print dress in a shade of green that seemed very becoming on her.

She glanced at Fox. "A new one?" she asked Leyra, who nodded.

"He just arrived today. He's docile enough that we decided he could fill the spot of collective personal assistant for the Alphas," Leyra explained. As she spoke, she gestured at the tray Fox still carried and pointed at the counter by the sink. Fox set it down.

"Hm," the other woman hummed in interest, looking right at Fox without even trying to be inconspicuous about it. Fox watched as she took in his appearance. He wondered if she saw all the same things Leyra had seen. Fox took this chance to scrutinize her a little more, too.

She wasn't as built as Leyra, her thighs and arms softer, but not skinny. Her knees and palms seemed calloused, and Fox wondered if she was a gardener or a cleaner. Judging by the plants he saw scattered around the house, and the smell of flowers in the kitchen windowsill, she was probably the former. He noticed that she also had a tattoo of a starling on her forearm. Fox realized, just then, that these two were mates.

"I'm Sunshine," she greeted, and held out a hand for Fox to shake. Fox glanced warily at Leyra, but she wasn't glaring a warning at him, so he tentatively reached out and shook her hand.

"I'm Fox," he replied. He took his hand back the moment her gentle grip loosened.

Sunshine smiled at him, a wide and warm thing, and Fox felt slightly flustered at such a sight. He turned his gaze to the floor. "Where will he be staying?" Sunshine asked.

"One of our spare rooms until a bunker opens up," Leyra said. "Are you comfortable with him staying here, or do you want one of the others to take him?"

Sunshine shrugged, still smiling. "Here is fine. If he gives off any bad vibes, we can move him," she said. Fox couldn't help but raise his brows at the notion of staying in someone's house. A real, sturdy house that looked and smelled like a home. It had been a long time since Fox had gotten to stay anywhere like this. He was used to camping, motels, sheds, cells, sometimes even up in trees. If he was lucky, he found a vacation cabin, but that was the closest thing he got to a comfy shelter, and he could never stay there for very long.

Fox wanted to ask how long it might be for a bunker to open up, how long he'd be permitted to stay in this house, but he couldn't find his voice. Leyra turned to him. "I'll show you your room, then."

Fox followed her through the house again, up a set of stairs where a vine plant was growing around the banister, and down a small hallway. They passed a bathroom, which Leyra pointed out as the guest's bathroom and was free for him to use. Fox's mind reeled some more at the promise of getting to shower in warm water. Not much farther down from the bathroom, Leyra opened a door to a plain room, with only a queen bed and a small dresser.

Fox stared at the bed. Two plush pillows, one thick brown comforter, one knitted patterned blanket. He felt like this was too much to allow a lone wolf to use.

"Here it is. And here's the rules. No funny business, no stashes, no sneaking out through the window like a teenager. I don't want to catch you roaming the house while we're sleeping. You come and go with permission only, and you ask before helping yourself to anything in the house. That includes food. I swear, if I catch you stealing anything from us, your ass is getting a hard whooping and you'll never get to stay in anyone's house here again. You'll sleep outside until a bunker opens up. Am I making myself clear?" Leyra said.

"Yes ma'am," Fox replied immediately. He didn't want to know what it felt like to get a beating from her. "I understand."

He still couldn't take his eyes off the bed. He could feel Leyra staring hard at the side of his head. "How- how long until a bunker opens up?" he finally managed to ask.

"Until one of the other lone wolves dies," Leyra replied. She didn't care to sugar coat it. This caught Fox's attention.

"Dies?" he repeated.

"That's the only way a lone wolf leaves here. You mess up enough times, you're executed. You get into a nasty fight to the death and lose, that's it. You try to leave, you'll be hunted down." She said it so matter of factly, Fox wondered if she had any warmth in her heart. She must have some, if she had a mate like Sunshine, but it was probably very little. Fox didn't think he would enjoy living with her.

"I see..." he replied, turning his gaze away from her strong unwavering one. "Mess up how?" he asked.

"Theft, fighting, attempting to escape, disobeying enough orders. You get the idea," she answered. Fox nodded. He curled his toes against the carpet.

"There's a laundry bin in the closet; you're expected to clean your clothes yourself. Keep that bathroom clean, too," Leyra added. Fox nodded again, with a whispered polite acknowledgment.

The two of them stood there for a long moment, Fox unsure if he was allowed to break away or await an order, and Leyra simply studying him.

"What's West?" she asked at length. It took a second for Fox to understand where the question came from, but when he remembered, he sighed.

"Just... a bucket list destination," he said. It was a partial truth.

"Oh. Where to?" Leyra asked, sounding interested.

"Redwood National Park," he said.

"I've heard that's a good one. Very touristy though," she replied. Fox grew a little skeptical and confused by this small talk, after all the information she just gave him.

"I think most national parks are," he mumbled. She nodded agreement.

"It's late, so you can turn in for now. Tomorrow you'll be given a tour, and then a rundown of what's going to be expected of you," she said.

"Okay," Fox replied, and stepped into his room. Leyra turned and left him alone, heading back downstairs.

Fox looked at the bed again. It looked clean and untouched, and the idea of lying down in it reminded him of how filthy he was. He just remembered he had lost his pack of belongings when he'd gotten captured; it had been confiscated before he was dragged to the hole. He wondered if the Betas had thrown his stuff away or taken it somewhere for holding. He hoped he could get it back, because that's where all his toiletries and clothes were.

Fox went back downstairs. He found Leyra and Sunshine in the kitchen. "Excuse me," he said, and they turned to look at him. "Would it be possible to get my bag back?"

"Oh right," Leyra said. "Come with me, we'll go get it." She started forward, and Fox felt a rush of relief at knowing his things hadn't been discarded. Leyra led him over to a garage door, grabbing a set of car keys from a hook on the wall. They descended a couple stairs into the garage, and Leyra pressed a button on the wall, and the garage began to open.

She gestured to the passenger door as the lights flashed on a sleek black suv, the car doors unlocking. The two of them climbed into the car, and Leyra pulled out of the garage. Fox was glad they were taking a sheltered method of travel, because the light sprinkling outside had quickly turned into a steady downpour.

Rain beat against the roof of the car, and Leyra turned on her windshield wipers. Fox watched the road as she drove down the dirt path, away from the four big houses and down the hill through the trees. It was starting to get a little darker outside, which filled Fox with a sense of anxiety. He reminded himself that he didn't have to rush to build a warm and dry shelter tonight, that he already had one provided for him.

Leyra drove down out of the trees onto a more solid asphalt road. Fox calculated that it took about five minutes to drive into town, the trees dispersing and buildings taking their place. They passed by a gas station, a liquor store, a grocery store, a hardware store, all normal things you would find in any other town. The roads were wide, but only had one lane each way, and Fox noticed that the sidewalks were very wide and lined with well-lit lamps, as well as shrubs serving as partitions between the road and the sidewalk. It was both a drivable and walkable town.

Leyra didn't drive into the heart of town, luckily. Fox wanted to avoid getting gawked at, or humiliated. She turned into a small parking lot of an old building. It looked like a town hall or a bank, with its limestone material and arched windows.

Leyra parked, and the two of them got out and ducked their heads against the rain. Fox followed the Alpha inside.

The interior of the building struck him as more of a courthouse now, with muted sounds and thick wooden doors and marbled floors. "This way," Leyra said, and she took him down the entryway hall to a big set of stairs. They went up to the next floor, down another hall, and finally stopped at a door with a plaque labeled "Confiscated/Holdings".

Leyra searched through the keys she held in her hand and unlocked the door. Inside, a Beta sat immediately to their right, behind a desk. Fox avoided looking at him.

"Oh, Alpha Leyra. What can I help you find?" the Beta asked.

"This one's bag," Leyra replied, pointing a thumb over her shoulder at Fox.

"Ah," the Beta responded, his tone suggesting that he easily recognized Fox. "His stuff is in locker 12."

"Thanks," Leyra said. The Beta stood up and took them down a row of lockers. There were a lot of them, arranged like bookshelves in a library. All of them either had key locks or combination locks, or both. They stopped in front of locker 12, where the Beta spun a dial to unlock it. Fox anxiously awaited for the door to open, and he let out a breath of reassurance as he laid eyes on his bag.

It was a tattered thing, rumpled and stained and patched in some places, a few loose threads coming off the straps. Fox reached his hand forward to grab it, then stopped halfway. He looked at Leyra, uncertain.

She reached forward for him and grabbed his bag, handing it to him. Fox gratefully took it and hugged it to his chest. He turned around and crouched down on the floor, unzipping the bag and searching through its contents to make sure all of his things were still there.

Three pairs of clothes were still there. His jacket was still there. His travel bag of toiletries were there. His tin box of knickknacks and mementos of his travels over the years, where he kept magnets and pins and photos and keychains of various places he had visited, was still there, sitting buried at the bottom. His giant water bottle/thermos was still there, unopened. His collection of paper maps was still tucked in the same pocket it had been in before. He still had his compass, his fire starter, his camping tarp, and even his Swiss Army knife. Not even his meager roll of cash had been taken.

"Are you done?" Leyra asked when Fox finally paused in his search. He figured they would have taken the valuable things, and especially his Swiss Army knife, but everything was still there.

"Yes..." Fox mumbled, and stood, hugging his bag to his chest again.

"We looked through it, but didn't take anything. We don't condone theft, even if it belongs to a lone wolf. Just don't make us regret letting you keep that knife tool, because we will take it if you use it to hurt someone," the Beta told him. Fox didn't want to meet his gaze, but he was grateful for their unexpected gesture of kindness.

"Thanks. And I won't," he said.

"Good," Leyra said, then sighed heavily. She was probably tired. "Let's head back, then."

They drove back to Leyra's house. It was thoroughly dark by the time they got back, and lightning was starting to flash across the sky, booming thunder following close behind. The moment they were back inside the warm, sturdy house, Fox went upstairs to shower.

3, Alpha Evander

The bathroom was spotless and dustless. The sink had enough counter space on both sides that Fox could set his bag down on one. The mirror spanned most of the wall above the sink, but Fox merely spared himself a glance. He knew how much dirt and grime covered his sunburned-then-suntanned skin, and he didn't care to refresh his memory on how disheveled his dark brown hair had grown, or how devoid of emotion his hazel eyes had become, or how easy it was to spot the pale lines of various scars on his body, or how lean he had grown after a life with scarce food. Looking at himself for too long only made him ache deep inside.

The shower had a decently sized bathtub in it, without a hint of mold. The curtain sported a generic mountain design, and there was a lone painting hung on the wall above the towel rack, which had both a body towel and a hand towel already draped over it. Fox smiled a little at the sight.

He unzipped his bag and took out a pair of clothes. The closest thing he had to pajamas were some sweatpants and a thermal long sleeve. He set them aside.

He figured out the faucet in the shower, and waited for the spray to turn warm. When it did, he eagerly stepped in and groaned softly as the water rushed over him. Fox hadn't had a warm shower since his last stay at a motel, about two months ago, and that shower hadn't been nearly as nice as this one.

Fox took his time washing his hair and his body, making sure to scrub every inch, until he didn't feel so grimy anymore. Then he took some time to simply bask in the warmth, letting the steam fill his lungs and the gentle drumming of the water massage his shoulders.

When the water turned tepid, he shut it off and stepped out to dry. He used the towel to scrub himself dry enough to put on his sleepwear, and then he brushed his teeth. When he felt thoroughly freshened up and cleaned, he gathered his things back in his bag and left to go to his room.

Fox felt strange calling it his room. He knew it was a temporary residence, but he was allowed to have that space all to himself, and it was a funny feeling. He felt both nostalgic and out of place. He pushed away the memories that tried to rise as a result of those feelings. Reminiscing never did him any good. Those memories only ever served to hurt him.

Fox shut the door behind him. A calmness settled in him then, the notion of privacy soothing his nerves. He set his bag down on the floor by the bed, and wasted no time climbing under the covers.

The mattress accepted his weight with ease. The pillows were soft and cradled his head just right. The duvet was cozy, just the right amount of heavy to keep him comfortable. Fox couldn't help the groan that escaped him. His body relaxed in a way it hadn't been able to for a long time, his muscles going slack, and his subconscious alertness shutting down for the night.

Despite Alpha Leyra's hardness, and the threat of what this pack could do to him if he stepped too far out of line, Fox felt safe like this. Alone in this room, with a bed and bathroom all to himself. Put in perspective, it was so simple, but it was everything to Fox.

He fell asleep to the sound of pattering rain and rumbling thunder, the flashes of lightning outside hardly enough to rouse him.

Fox had one of the best sleeps he'd had in years. He woke to a sunny but damp morning, his body feeling thoroughly rested. Fox almost felt like he was being pampered, but then he remembered where he was, whose house he was in, and he reminded himself not to let all this luxury get to his head. It could be taken away in a heartbeat.

Fox remembered that today he was being given a tour. Dread and anxiety filled his chest, and he stubbornly stayed in bed for as long as he was allowed.

Which lasted until ten in the morning. Someone knocked on his door, a nod to his privacy that Fox hadn't been expecting. He reluctantly rose from the warm covers and trudged over to the door. He opened it to find Sunshine standing there.

She beamed at him, and Fox was once again flustered by such a friendly smile. He turned his gaze to her feet, where he noticed her toenails were painted blue. "There's breakfast downstairs. Leyra would like you to join us."

Fox nodded. He trailed after Sunshine as she headed downstairs, her long black skirt billowing around her ankles. The smell of eggs and bacon filled his nose, growing stronger the closer he got. His mouth was watering by the time he reached the kitchen, where breakfast was set up on their small circle dining table.

Fox pulled out a chair and sat down. "Good morning," Leyra greeted, who was already sat and had a huge serving of waffles, eggs, and bacon on her plate. Sunshine began to pile a smaller, more reasonable portion on her plate.

"Good morning," Fox greeted in return. He felt unsure if it was alright for him to help himself. Leyra noticed his hesitation.

"You can have some. But don't expect this all the time," she said. Fox nodded with a whispered thanks, and cautiously divied up some bacon and eggs for himself. He noticed a full glass of water was already filled at his spot.

As he ate, he tried to figure out what to make of this. Just yesterday he was being given a choice of warm food or half-eaten scraps, and today he was being offered warm food and clean water without any bargaining at all. Fox had a feeling that the other lone wolves weren't having a breakfast like this. He didn't know what that meant for him, if this was a good sign or a bad one.

He chewed his food slowly and with his head ducked. He made sure to eat every bite and drink every drop, and he said his thanks again when he was done. He wanted to have more, but he didn't want to come across to them the wrong way. He felt if he helped himself to more, they would think he was a little too comfortable, and might do something to take him down a peg.

Leyra was still eating her giant portion. Sunshine was finishing hers off. Fox wanted to ask the Alpha a question, but felt it might be rude to interrupt her eating. He tucked his hands under his thighs and waited.

Fortunately, he didn't have to wait for long. "Today you'll properly meet the other three Alphas and get to know what each of our duties entail. Then we'll give you a general tour of our territory so you have an idea of where to go in case you need to run errands. After that, we'll see who needs your assistance first," Leyra told him.

Fox nodded, glad that his question was answered without him having to ask it. It occurred to him that, with a territory this big, running errands all on foot was probably going to take him a while. There was no way an Alpha here would let him borrow their car. Maybe he'd be allowed a bike with a basket.

"You can go get changed. Meet me down here when you're done," Leyra said. Fox slid out of his chair and went back upstairs. He changed into a pair of black jeans and a navy long sleeve. He took a peek out the window to see the sky was still partially cloudy. He didn't want to get caught in any rain with no protection, so he took his jacket with him.

He stopped in the bathroom to brush his teeth again. Then he tucked all his belongings in his bag and hid it in his closet. Then he returned downstairs and took his shoes out from their hiding spot, slipping them on. He sat on the little bench by the front door and waited. Alpha Leyra jogged down the stairs about five minutes later.

She had on an activewear outfit, like she was about to go work out. She gestured to Fox without a word, and the two of them left the house.

"The four of us cover four main clusters," Leyra began as they walked down the dirt road. "I oversee hunts and food distribution, as well as making sure everyone has a job that contributes to the pack. Alpha Ahren oversees pack morale, committees and recreational facilities. He makes sure everyone is happy, and settles disputes and keeps records of areas that need improvement. Alpha Evander oversees discipline, fight training, and border patrol. He's the one who makes sure everyone knows their place, and there's no insurrection, rebellion, or anything even close to resembling a gang. The lone wolves are mainly under his jurisdiction. And Alpha Rishima oversees everything else. Schooling, the medical sector, town businesses, things like that."

Fox listened carefully, not wanting to miss any important information. They neared one of the other large houses. The one they approached was painted a calm sea blue and had a very big porch with an awning and outdoor heaters. There were four chairs circled around a big fire pit in the backyard, as well as a volleyball net and a swimming pool.

"Each Alpha has at least three Betas to help them with their duties, but there's still a lot on everyone's plate. This is why you're going to be our shared assistant-slash-servant," Leyra said as they walked up to the front door. Leyra knocked a couple times, but then opened the door anyway and let herself in. Fox stepped in behind her, wary.

Fox immediately smelled three other Alphas in the house. He wasn't expecting all of them to be here, and his shoulders grew tense. They walked into a small front living room, which only had a few armchairs and a coffee table. Leyra kept walking, heading through a doorway and around the corner into a wider room, where one side was a bigger living room with an entertainment center, and the other side was a big kitchen with both an island counter, a bar, and a big dining table. A set of sliding glass doors opened out into the backyard.

The other Alphas were spaced out in this room. Fox stared at the floor, not daring to look at anyone directly.

"Leyra. About time," one of the males greeted, tone disgruntled and annoyed.

"Cállate, Evander. Like you haven't taken your sweet time before," Leyra responded. She was easily absorbed into the group, the others turning their attention to her and adjusting their body language to include her. Fox, however, stayed by the doorway, hiding part of himself behind the frame.

"I see you brought the mute. Has he caused you any trouble?" Evander asked. Fox vaguely started to recognize his voice as the Alpha who had repeatedly asked him his name, and then stated he could rot in the hole.

"No. He's been completely obedient so far. I told you he was docile," Leyra answered. Fox grew rigid as he saw a pair of feet walk over to him.

"Until he's not," Evander said. He reached out and took Fox's jaw in his hand, angling his face up so Fox was forced to meet his gaze. Fox met skeptical and hard blue eyes, light eyebrows furrowed in a scowl. His skin was white but suntanned, and he had slightly hollow cheeks and dusty brown hair that was shaved on the sides and back, and left to grow a few inches long on top. He towered a half foot taller over Fox, and he matched Leyra in terms of musculature and scarring. Fox knew that one punch from this werewolf would send him flying.

"Are you going to start answering the questions I ask you?" Evander asked in a slight growl. Fox swallowed, willing the small tremors in his legs to stop. He tried to answer, but he had lost his voice again. Fear kept his mouth shut.

He heard Leyra sigh. "Answer him," she said. Fox swallowed again.

"Yes, sir," he whispered. One of Evander's eyebrows rose, his expression turning from a scowl into vague intrigue.

"Obedient and polite," he mused, leaning away from Fox and releasing his jaw.

"I told you," Leyra said.

"We'll see how long that holds up," Evander replied, not completely convinced. Fox slowly exhaled the breath he'd been holding.

"Who's he shadowing first?" the other male Alpha, Ahren, asked.

Just as Fox was silently pleading for it not to be Evander, Evander said, "I could use him today. We're evaluating new recruits."

"Alright. He still needs a tour, though," Leyra said.

"I'll show him around my sectors. You guys can tour him around yours," Evander replied. Leyra shrugged, unperturbed. Fox felt like he was being handed over to the police.

"Fine by me," Rishima said. Evander turned to leave, picking up a binder with a ton of papers inside from the kitchen counter.

"Come on then, Fox," he said, and Fox forced his feet to trail after him.

The two of them exited the house, and Evander led the way across the field to some unknown destination. Evander had a long stride, and Fox had to walk a little faster than his usual pace to keep up.

They headed into the trees. The path they took was narrow and tread-worn. It took them a while to traverse through the woods, and Fox expected Evander to strike up conversation like Leyra had, but he kept quiet. Evander didn't seem too interested in Fox and his backstory, and that relieved Fox.

Eventually, they broke out of the woods and walked out onto yet another field. This field, however, had what looked like an obstacle course, starting from one end of the field and arching around the perimeter to the other end. There was a building that looked like a concessions stand with a handful of benches beside it, where Fox could see a group of young men and women sitting and eating. There was also a big sand pit that two males were wrestling each other on, a group of onlookers cheering them on.

Evander held up a palm, not turning to look at Fox. "The training sector," he stated.

The group of werewolves noticed Evander's approach and began to stand up, giving him their attention.

Fox held back at this point, slowing his steps until he was a good distance away from the big group. He watched as Evander came to a stop, crossing his arms and watching the two males wrestle in the sand.

The group of werewolves swiveled their heads between Evander and the wrestlers, probably unsure if they should intervene and tell the wrestlers to stop and stand at attention. Fox studied Evander. He couldn't tell if the Alpha was waiting for the wrestling to stop, or if he was scrutinizing the way they were fighting.

Fox watched the wrestling match. One male kept his legs spread at a wide stance and was partially crouched, using his center of gravity as an aid to not get knocked over. The other male kept trying to get his arms around his opponent's leg to trip him up, but his stance made it difficult.

Eventually, after some obvious struggling, the male with the wide stance grabbed the other male's arm and twisted it around, shifting his feet to catch the other male's ankle, and used both leverage points to shove the other male to the ground. He landed with a hefty grunt, and the other male pinned his knee to his chest. The one on the ground struggled, trying to get his opponent's weight off him, but to no avail. After a few failed attempts, he slapped the sand and growled. "Tap, tap."

Evander clapped a few times, which finally caught both wrestlers' attention. They whipped their heads around and realized who had arrived, and quickly scrambled up to their feet.

"That was good form. What's your name?" Evander asked the victor.

"Luke, sir," he responded. The other werewolf had an embarrassed blush on his cheeks and neck, probably not happy about losing in front of one of his Alphas.

"Luke. Take a spot back in the sand pit. And you," Evander said, pointing to the loser, "go sit down over there." He pointed to an open spot in the grass on one side of the sand pit. The loser complied with an unhappy sigh. Evander turned to the group.

"Each one of you is going to take a turn wrestling. Whoever wins stays in the pit to go another round, whoever loses sits down over there with him. If you manage to win three times before being bested, you take a seat over there." Evander pointed to the other side of the sand pit.

The group collectively nodded their understanding. "Alright. You're going first," Evander said, pointing to a random werewolf in the group.

The matches began. Fox waited off to the side, keeping an eye on both Evander and the other werewolves. At one point, Evander seemed to remember that Fox was there. "Fox, go in the snack shack and help the other lone wolf with stocking and cleaning. I won't need you two until after this."

Fox didn't want to say anything, but he didn't want to make Evander angry at him, so he responded with a quiet "Yes, sir," and headed over to the concessions stand.

He opened the door that read "staff" and entered. Fox felt like he was hit in the face by a wall of scents, varying from salt to sugar to bread to meat. He paused and swallowed down the sudden buildup of saliva in his mouth, willing himself not to eat anything without Evander's permission. He didn't want to experience a punishment from him.

The snack shack was mostly one big room, with a couple fryers, a fridge, a freezer, an ice machine, and a couple tabletop ovens. Straight ahead at the other end of the building, he spotted another lone wolf leaning against the counter of the ordering window, watching the wrestling match. He had blond hair that looked like it needed to be brushed, and white skin with a sunburned neck and arms. He wore a plain gray shirt and jeans. Fox noticed a black band around his neck, like a collar or choker.

"Um, hello," Fox greeted. The other wolf bolted upright and turned around. His caught-red-handed expression relaxed when he saw Fox, and Fox saw the rest of the band around his neck. It was a shock collar.

"Hello. You're the newbie, aren't you?" he replied. At the term, Fox wondered how quickly news of his capture had spread throughout the pack. He wondered how many knew of his specific position, and whether or not it was a bad thing for them to know.

Fox nodded. The other wolf looked him up and down, his visage not betraying any inner opinions on Fox, which made Fox wary. "I'm Seb," he said.

"I'm Fox," Fox replied. Seb raised a brow, like many people did when they heard Fox's name, but he didn't comment on it.

"You here to help with concessions?" Seb asked.

"Alpha Evander told me to clean and stock," Fox said. Seb waved a hand at an open closet where cleaning supplies were kept. Fox could see a broom, dustpan, mop, a stack of rags, and a couple cleaning chemicals.

"Cleaning stuff is there." He waved a hand up towards the ceiling, where Fox saw a bunch of high shelves with boxes stacked on top. "Cups and plates and whatever are up there."

Fox nodded again. He swept his gaze around the space to see where he should start. He decided to grab some rags and start wiping down surfaces.

As he worked, silent and minding his business, he noticed Seb was just standing there, watching him, not minding his business. Fox did his best to ignore it, but after a while, he began to grow a little suspicious of Seb's intentions. He stopped cleaning and looked right at him.

"What?" Fox asked. Seb tilted his head a bit.

"You're really making sure it's spotless, huh? Why are you putting that much effort into following Alpha Douchebag's orders?" Seb asked.

"I don't want to get into trouble," Fox told him.

Seb snickered a little, his eyebrows tilting up to form an expression of pity on his face. "He's gonna beat you up anyway."

Fox's shoulders tensed. "Why? I'm doing what he told me to."

"That's what he does. It doesn't matter how well you behave, he looks for ways to trip us up and punish us. It's his way of reminding us that we're below everyone else here," Seb stated. "We don't have rights like everyone else. Sure, we get little prizes for good behavior, but it doesn't last long. Evander doesn't want us getting comfortable or thinking we're finally getting accepted."

"Why?" Fox asked again. "What's so bad about accepting us if we're doing good?"

Seb shrugged. "Fuck if I know," he said unhelpfully.

Fox didn't understand. Why would this pack keep their trespassers from leaving? Why would they reward them for good behavior, but never fully accept them if they kept being good? Why would Alpha Evander purposely look for ways to beat the lone wolves back down into the dirt? If Leyra was so concerned about the lone wolves snapping or panicking and hurting her pack members, why keep the potential threats around? Or why not help them regulate their issues?

Fox had a feeling that he had a lot to figure out about Lily of the Valley Pack.

But even despite this revelation, Fox continued to do what he'd been told to do. Seb watched him think for a moment, and then turn and pick up the broom to sweep. Seb scoffed in disbelief. He shook his head and turned to watch the wrestling matches again.

Fox didn't care to pay attention to the werewolves outside. He just narrowed his line of sight down to the task in front of him. This pack didn't yet make sense to him, but he had learned from dozens of other packs he'd encountered; Alphas were the kind of wolves who demanded respect and obedience, and if he complied, they tended to go a little easier on him. Even if Evander would cook up some excuse to keep putting him in his place, Fox hoped that obeying his orders would make his punishments less severe. It had worked for him enough times in the past.

So Fox scrubbed every surface that looked remotely dirty. He cleaned the windows and stainless steel. He swept and mopped the floors, twice. He opened the boxes on the shelves and stocked the plastic cups and paper plates and disposable utensils and napkins, and he broke down the clumping ice in the ice machine, and organized the food stored in the freezers and fridges, and even changed the trash, leaving the full bag over by the door, out of the way.

By the end of his chores, Fox was thirsty. Seb was still distracted by the wrestling, and Evander was out of sight, so Fox secretly took a cup and filled it with water. He looked at Seb again, who was still not paying attention to him, but Fox didn't want to risk it. He tucked himself behind a fridge, hiding, and gulped down the water like Evander was about to open the door and catch him.

He tossed his cup, pushing it as far down into the trash as possible. He looked around for anything more he could do, but everything was as good as it could get. Tentatively, he inched closer to Seb so he could look out the ordering window and see the progress outside.

It seemed like only two matches were left, with one in progress. There was a sizable amount of werewolves sitting on the loser's side, and only about ten on the winner's side. Fox leaned forward a bit to see Evander making notes in the binder he brought with him.

When the matches finally finished, Evander told everyone to run four laps around the obstacle course. There were some groaning and grumbling amongst the group, but Evander growled loud and clear, and any disgruntled protesting ceased, and everyone obeyed.

Evander turned to the concession stand. Fox tensed and backed away from Seb, looking around for any last minute fixes he could make. Seb stood up all the way and leaned back against the counter with his arms crossed, looking far less stressed than Fox felt.

The door to the shack opened, and Fox froze. The Alpha swept his gaze around the building, taking in its state of cleanliness, and his eyebrows rose a bit in mild surprise. "Hmm. This looks a lot better than I was expecting." He turned his gaze to Fox and Seb. "The two of you did this together?"

Seb was very quick to answer. "Yep. I cleaned everything and Fox stocked."

Fox gave him a sharp look, almost glaring, but he didn't want to start a fight, so he looked at his feet. Evander was silent for a moment, long enough to set Fox's nerves off.

"Really?" Evander asked. His low tone revealed that he was not fooled at all. "Fox?"

Fox's lips parted, but Seb interjected. "Yeah, we did rock paper scissors on it."

"Is your fucking name Fox?" Evander growled. Seb shifted his stance, nervous.

Fox wrung his fingers together in a fidget. "Um, I... we..." he glanced warily at Seb, who was harshly side-eying him. Evander stepped forward, and Fox flinched and backed up against the fridge.

"Don't look at him," Evander ordered. He put himself between the two, his gaze narrowed on Fox. "He's not here right now. I am asking you. Did the two of you do this together?"

Fox swallowed. He could pick two sides here, the lone wolf or the Alpha. If he picked the lone wolf, he would get on the Alpha's bad side and be seen as a liar and in league with the other lone wolves, which would put him on everyone's bad side, except for the lone wolves. If he picked the Alpha's side, he would win points with the four of them and be seen as somewhat loyal to them, but he would be labeled as a snitch and an enemy by the lone wolves, and if they were conniving enough, they could scheme to thwart Fox's livelihood here, or attempt to seriously hurt him behind closed doors.

Fox had experience with both. He knew that loyalty to an Alpha had far more long lasting benefits than loyalty to a lone wolf. Alphas had changed their opinion of him, had treated him halfway decent instead of terrible, and had given him freedom instead of death. Lone wolves were hit or misses; they would either decide against stealing his stuff while he slept, or they would take advantage of his attempt at good will and screw him over, landing him in precarious situations while the other lone wolf got away.

Fox didn't know Seb at all. He didn't know what Seb would do if he sided with him or not. Fox risked more if he sided with him. He was nearly guaranteed benefits if he sided with Evander, even if that meant the lone wolves turning on him.

In conclusion, it was an easy choice to make. Fox needed to look out for himself, because in the end, he was always the only one left.

"No, sir..." Fox whispered. He could hear Seb stifle a snarl under his breath.

"Am I right in assuming that you did all this, by yourself," Evander responded, gesturing widely to the snack shack. "And this lazy fuck," Evander turned and pointed to the floor where Seb stood, "stood here and did jack shit the entire time?"

Fox could feel the growing irritation in Evander's body, so he couldn't bring himself to look at his face. His gaze was where he was pointing, and that was how he noticed that the spot Seb stood in was the only dirty spot on the entire floor. Fox hadn't wanted to tell him to move while he was mopping, and Seb hadn't bothered lifting his feet, so he had mopped around him and left that one spot dirty.

Fox hadn't realized what a stark difference there was between the dirty spot and the rest of the newly cleaned floor. That was part of how Evander knew Seb was lying.

"Y-Yes, yes sir," Fox stammered quietly. Evander exhaled in a very aggressive manner, and turned to leave the shack.

"Come here, both of you," he commanded. Fox eyed Seb, who was glaring daggers at him.

"You little..." he fumed, his teeth growing sharp as he bared them at Fox.

"Now!" Evander yelled over his shoulder. Fox scurried to obey. Seb snarled behind him, and the next thing he knew he was being tackled to the ground.

Teeth bit into his shoulder, and instinct took over. Fox twisted and snarled and scratched at the wolf on top of him, who bit down hard on his shoulder and tugged, thrashing his head, trying to rip a chunk free, his clawed hands digging into Fox's chest.

As soon as it started, the two of them were ripped apart by a pair of strong hands. Fox yelped and whined as he felt Seb's teeth tear through his flesh. The hand that had hold of his neck threw him outside, where he tumbled onto the grass. He groaned as his shoulder and chest throbbed.

"You little snitch!" Seb yelled, but he grunted right after as Evander socked him in the gut and threw him ten feet away.

"Shut it, Seb! You ratted yourself out!" Evander snapped. The sudden attack from the lone wolf and the intense amount of dominance radiating off the Alpha left Fox trembling, shocked and afraid at once as the adrenaline partially faded. He did the only thing that could keep him safe at that moment, which was curl into a ball with his arms tucked between his legs and his hands covering his head.

He stayed that way as he listened to Evander beat Seb. It wasn't a long beating, just a few punches with Seb crying out from each heavy hit.

Fox couldn't imagine how much those punches hurt, and he started to tremble more as he awaited his turn.

"Alright, recruits!" he heard Evander shout. "We're going to see how well you do with fighting a lone wolf."

Fox listened as the recruits slowly stopped running and formed a group again. He heard feet scuff the grass, growing closer to where he was crouched on the ground, and tensed every muscle in his body in preparation.

Fox felt a boot nudge his side. Not a kick, just a nudge. "Get up," Evander ordered. The aggression in his voice had toned way down. He didn't sound as upset with Fox as he had been with Seb.

Fox had to force his body to unfold, not wanting any hesitation to come across as disobedience. He uncurled shakily, his limbs feeling weak. His heart was pounding in his chest for a different reason now. He didn't want to fight over thirty werewolves.

"I'm sorry, Alpha," he whispered, struggling to stand.

"Just come on," Evander replied, tucking his boot under Fox's leg and nudging him again. His tone wasn't impatient, however. Fox gritted his teeth and pushed himself up to his feet.

He couldn't look anywhere but the ground. Evander grabbed the back of his neck and hauled him over to the other werewolves.

Seb was doubled over on the ground, an arm tucked around his stomach and his other hand cradling his head. He slid a death glare over at Fox, and Fox avoided it.

"Losers of the wrestling matches, you'll be taking turns fighting Fox," Evander announced. "And the winners will be fighting Seb."

Fox wondered if this was Evander's twisted version of kindness.

The group of werewolves split into two. Evander hauled Fox over to a clear spot in the field, away from Seb and the winners, and instructed everyone to form a line. Evander dragged some spare sandbags and placed them in four spots, spaced out to form a square in the grass.

"Stand there," he told Fox, and Fox reluctantly complied, taking post on one side of the makeshift square.

Evander went over to the other group and did the same with them. "Here are the rules. You can hit and kick and mimic scratching and biting, but do not use your claws or fangs. When the lone wolf hits the ground and stays down for five seconds, you've won."

The Alpha went back to pick up his binder from where he dropped it in the grass. Then he picked a spot between the two sparring groups to watch. "Begin."

The bite wound in his shoulder was aching, throbbing, and the cuts in his chest were stinging fiercely. Fox hated fighting. He hated not knowing which move would be his last. He hated getting trapped or pinned down and not being able to escape. He hated the taste of someone else's blood in his mouth. He hated the feeling of tendons catching under his claws. He hated stitching himself up afterwards. He hated the feeling of knuckles on his head and in his gut.

As the first werewolf stepped up, a well built woman who was a foot shorter than him, Fox tried to shut out the pain in his body. He focused on her hands as she raised them up in fists by her face. She waited for him to make a move, but Fox just stood there. The tremors were gone. He accepted his position.

She swung. He ducked. She followed up with a kick. He dodged it. She swung again, one two, and he leapt back, one two.

She glanced at Evander. The Alpha just stood there and watched, face set in expressionless observation. She swung again, and Fox threw his arms up so she caught his forearms instead of his jaw.

She growled and tried to land a punch on his injured shoulder. Fox twisted to the side just in time for her to only graze his bicep. The rest of the fight went like this, her attempting to hit him, and Fox twisting or skittering out of the way.

"Enough. Next wolf," Evander ordered when it was obvious the fight was going nowhere. The woman exhaled heavily in frustration, glaring at Fox as she stormed out of the makeshift square. A male took her place. He was taller than Fox, but the same weight.

The fight went the same way. This male attempted to land as many hits and kicks as possible, but Fox either dodged them or used his thighs and arms as shields to protect his face and stomach.

Evander ended the fight when two minutes of no progress passed. The next wolf was also male, but heavier set, and he didn't attempt to hit right away, but instead bulldozed right into Fox and sent Fox sprawling to the ground. He landed with a grunt, but wasted no time in curling up like an armadillo and using his limbs as shields. The male whaled on him, hitting and kicking his shins and arms, catching his sides a few times, but Fox kept curled up tight and endured it.

"Enough, it's been more than five seconds. Next wolf," Evander said.

The rest of the fights went on like this. Distantly, Fox could hear Seb getting the same treatment, but he was clearly trying to fight back. Fox absently noticed that anytime Seb was getting too violent for the winners, Evander would press a button on a small remote in his hands, and the shock collar around Seb's neck would go off, subduing him.

Seb's fights ended sooner than Fox's, only because he had less opponents. Fox kept up his shield of limbs, dodging when he could, letting himself get tackled or bulldozed again and again and staying curled up anytime he was on the ground. He never tried to fight back. He just took whatever landed and tried to avoid the rest.

By the end of it, he was covered in bruises and aching all over. When Evander finally called it quits, Fox dropped to his sore knees and tried to catch his breath.

"Alright the lot of you, form a line for the obstacle course," Evander ordered. Fox peeked up through his sweaty hair to see Seb lying still on the ground, groaning softly.

Evander kicked Fox hard in the chest, sending him flying onto his back in a split second. Fox's breath got knocked out of him, and he laid there gasping, struggling to inhale. Evander watched with narrow displeased eyes.

"What kind of werewolf are you? I've never seen a wolf not try to defend themself against a threat. You should've snapped halfway through those fights," he said. "Every other lone wolf here would've given up your tactic. They would've fought back at some point."

Fox wanted to say that he didn't feel like any kind of werewolf, and it was the entire reason why he had renamed himself. But he was still struggling to breathe.

Evander waited. Fox finally managed to suck in a full breath, and he gasped as he rolled over onto his side. "I... I don't like fighting."

"You don't have to like it to do it," Evander bit out. "You think this timid act will last you forever?" He crouched down and grabbed a fistful of Fox's hair, using it to angle Fox's face up at him. Fox winced at the sting, unwillingly meeting Evander's gaze.

"You're going to snap eventually. And I'll be here when that day comes."

~Phew, this turned out longer than I expected

4, An Offer

Evander left them alone while the recruits ran the obstacle course. Fox stayed on the ground, keeping off his bitten shoulder and watching rain clouds pile up in the sky above him. It started to sprinkle a little bit at one point, but Evander didn't seem concerned about getting caught in a downpour.

The recruits finished up their laps around the obstacle course, and Evander told them to take a break.

"Seb, drag your sorry ass back inside the snack shack and start taking orders. And if you make a mess of Fox's cleanup job, you're getting another ass-whooping," Evander ordered the lone wolf. "Fox, you're coming with me to the med station."

At the sound of the word "med" Fox felt his heart rate quicken. Seb groaned and winced his way up to his feet, and began trudging away to the concessions building, his arms wrapped around his stomach.

He sent Fox a dirty look over his shoulder, but Evander caught it and released a loud warning growl. Seb turned away.

Seb had taken worse of a beating than Fox had, but maybe making him work instead of letting him rest was still part of Evander's punishment for him. Fox thought that fighting the winners of the wrestling matches had been enough of a punishment for simple laziness and lying, but maybe Evander didn't.

Fox heard Evander approach him where he still laid in the grass. The Alpha met Fox's wide-eyed gaze and sighed. "I've been informed that you have specific medical triggers," he stated. Fox just stared at him, feeling ice in his veins. Evander nudged his leg with his boot. "Up," he said.

Fox didn't want to, but he rolled over onto his knees and achingly rose to his feet. Evander began to walk over to a smaller building at the edge of the field, which had a red cross painted on its side. Fox shut his eyes as a memory flashed in his mind, begging for it not to grow vivid and intense.

Fox focused on putting one foot in front of the other, his gaze on the ground. He didn't look up when he reached the building with Evander. The Alpha opened the door, and Fox held his breath.

Evander turned on a light, illuminating a small medical room meant to hold at least two injured people and allow enough space for a caretaker to move around. There were two hospital beds and lots of shelves stocked with medical equipment.

The sight of it all caused a wave of nausea to roll through Fox's stomach. He shut his eyes again, his body already starting to tremble. He thought about rivers and skies instead of the memories from dark times, but he couldn't stop trembling.

Evander made some noise as he gathered some supplies. He paused at the door. "Are you not able to come in at all?" he asked. Fox vigorously shook his head.

"Fine. Sit down," the Alpha replied. Fox eased himself down onto the grass.

Evander closed the door behind him, and Fox let out his breath. The Alpha tossed a small hand towel at him. "Cover your nose with this," he said as a way of explanation.

Fox gratefully took it and covered the lower half of his face with it. Then Evander knelt down beside him and laid out his equipment. Fox stared hard at the trees in front of him. "Take your shirt off," Evander said. Fox complied, wincing as the fabric peeled away from his blood-crusted injuries. He covered his face with the towel again.

He heard the sloshing of liquid, then a burning sensation along his bite wound. Fox tensed and gritted his teeth, stifling a whine by tightly gripping his thigh instead. He could vaguely smell the antiseptic, and he balled up the towel around his nose as another wave of nausea rolled through his stomach.

Evander dabbed at the wound with a rag, cleaning up the blood. Each bit of pressure stung, but this wasn't anything new to Fox. In the grand view of all the injuries he'd ever gotten in his life, this wasn't the worst, and he was practiced with toughing it out.

"He got you pretty deep," Evander noted. "You'll need stitches."

Fox tried not to voice his dismay, but Evander seemed to be able to read it in his body language. "I'll numb you first," he said.

Fox waited as Evander went to retrieve a numbing solution. He pushed away memories of needles and tubes and fluids, attempting to distract himself by watching the dark gray and light gray clouds swirl above him, promising a heavier rainstorm later.

Evander returned. Fox made the mistake of glancing at him and flinched as he saw the Alpha holding a syringe. Panic flooded his veins and he whimpered, scooting away.

"Hey, easy," Evander said, voice gruff as he prepared to handle Fox's panic. Fox couldn't help it, he started shaking. He curled up and swallowed down the rising bile in his throat.

"No no no," Fox moaned quietly. Evander grabbed the back of his neck and forced his head down.

"Stay still and it'll be over in two seconds," he ordered. Fox's breathing started getting faster, shallower, and he yelped as he felt the needle enter his shoulder. Evander was quick to pin him down with his weight as Fox tried to thrash.

"Two seconds, see? You're fine," the Alpha said a moment later. He backed off of Fox, who was trying to swallow and inhale at the same time. He flinched when Evander thumped his back, his rough way of patting it.

The throbbing in his shoulder slowly died down as the numbing solution worked its magic. Fox repeated to himself again and again in his head that it was just a numbing agent, nothing sinister, nothing unknown, nothing experimental.

While Fox worked on controlling his inner panic, Evander stitched him up. He was quick but neat with it, probably from practice, and by the time he was done, Fox was calmer. Evander placed a gauze patch over the wound.

"You good now?" Evander asked as he watched Fox sit up from his hunched fetal position. Fox nodded mutely. "I still have to do your chest." Fox nodded again, tightening his grip on the towel covering his nose. He leaned back enough for Evander to clean out the cuts on his chest left by Seb's claws. The smell of the antiseptic was stronger here, and even with the towel blocking most of it, he still felt nauseous.

"Alpha?" Fox queried quietly, trying to distract himself again. Evander hummed short and gruff in reply. "Why did I have to fight?"

The Alpha sighed. "You did good with the task I asked you to complete, and you told me the truth about Seb instead of taking his side. But this is your first day here, and you need to know your place. You'll be rewarded for that good behavior, but you're still a lone wolf."

Fox cautiously met Evander's gaze. He could see distrust and low tolerance in his eyes, and Fox wondered how many lone wolves Evander has had to deal with. Fox understood now, though. He knew what lone wolves were like, and he knew that Evander only saw him as just another loner, albeit one with manners. Fox would have to work to prove to him that he was different, that he wasn't a threat or a problem.

Evander finished patching him up. Then he went inside the med shack to put the supplies away and wash his hands. As Fox waited, his gaze roamed around the bruises littering his arms and legs. He would be sore for the next couple days, but it could've been worse. Fox pulled his shirt back on just as the Alpha came back outside.

From then on, Fox was instructed to help Evander with setting up the rest of the training courses for the remainder of the evaluations. The new recruits would take short breaks, where they would get a drink from concessions or a snack to gain more calories. Evander filled his binder with notes, and by the time late afternoon rolled around, he finally called it quits.

The new recruits were dismissed, which was met with a chorus of relieved noises. Evander took a look inside the snack shack to see if Seb had made it dirty again. Aside from some stains on the counter-tops and some melted ice on the floor, it was decently clean. Evander dismissed Seb.

He turned to Fox. "Time for the rest of your tour," he said. Fox followed as the Alpha began walking off in a specific direction. He took Fox out of the field through the trees again. This walk took a lot longer, but Fox was used to walking for long periods of time, so it didn't bother him.

Evander showed him the holes in the ground that served as prison cells. They had four cells, each one in its own hole, and each one spaced out from each other. Each entrance to the holes were square metal doors on the ground, with grates for the sake of air ventilation. Fox didn't like being back here, remembering how dark and time-bending the hole had been for him.

Evander explained that they only kept one prisoner in each hole separately to avoid scheming, either for escape or for an attack. It was rare they ever had big groups of prisoners, though. Fox only half listened, too busy focusing on being grateful for the sky and daylight and fresh air.

Then Evander took him somewhere else, walking for a while again, traversing through more trees. Fox was realizing that a good majority of their territory was made up of forest, with very little adjustments to the plant life to make room for their human activities, hence why everything seemed to have its own designated field. Fox had to appreciate their concern for conservation.

Evander showed him their border patrol barracks, where a group of Betas and well-built fighter werewolves were stationed. Evander explained that here was where they traded shifts and randevoused for information exchange. Evander didn't take Fox inside to show him, but he said that they had a detailed map of their territory, and that whenever outside threats were detected, they would convene there to discuss defense tactics.

He turned to Fox and took his jaw in his hand, angling Fox's head up so he had to meet eyes with the Alpha. His gaze was intense and serious, and Fox wanted to pull away. "If I ever catch you here without an Alpha with you, or without an Alpha's permission, your ass is mine."

Fox shuddered at the growl in Evander's voice, the intense promise in his eyes. He knew a punishment from any Alpha would be hard to bear, but a serious punishment from Evander would probably land him in their medical sector.

"Yes, sir, I understand," Fox whispered in a strained voice. Evander let his jaw go.

Then Evander took him to their last stop: the lone wolves' bunkers.

Fox's stomach dropped as he laid eyes on them. There were ten in total, and they were situated similarly to the prison holes. Each one was separate, and two-thirds underground. Each one seemed to only have one long but extremely narrow window, not allowing for even the smallest werewolf to squeeze through, and it was right at ground level. Each bunker was made of cement, ensuring that digging was not a way out. The doors to get inside were slanted and small, almost similar to the square metal doors of the prison holes. And each bunker was very, very small.

There were a few Betas here as well, standing guard. They nodded to their Alpha as the two of them entered the field.

"You would've been assigned to one of these, but they're all full and can't accommodate two lone wolves. We wouldn't allow two lone wolves to stay together, anyway. Too big a risk of fights and scheming," Evander told Fox. As they walked around the bunkers,

Fox spotted a long picnic table in the middle of all the bunkers that was big enough to seat at least twelve people.

"Here is where they all have supervised meals. A lot of you tend to have food aggression," a fact Fox already knew "so each mealtime is supervised by a group of Betas or even myself, if I have time. Any fighting or stealing of someone else's food results in punishment. Each one of you has a decent amount of scraps and water, so there shouldn't be anyone left wanting. I would expect you to eat here, too, but it probably won't happen too often if you're spending every day with one of us Alphas."

Fox nodded to show he was listening. He was glad to hear that he wouldn't have to spend too much time here. He wanted to avoid the other lone wolves as much as possible. It seemed like most of them were out doing their assigned labor, but Seb was probably already back here in his own bunker.

As Fox stared at the cement huts half buried in the ground, he really hoped that nobody would be dying anytime soon.

"Okay, that's all for today. You can head back to Leyra's house for now. She might send you back here for dinner, though, so don't get too comfy there," Evander said.

"Yes, sir," Fox said. He looked around and discovered that he didn't really have a clue on where to go to get back to the Alphas' houses. "Which- which way do I go?" he asked.

Evander pointed at a worn path in the trees. Fox was noticing a pattern with that, too. "Just take that all the way there. It's not too far. This place and our houses are kept fairly close, mainly so we can keep a close eye on all of you and so we can get here quickly if anything happens."

Fox nodded again, and he set off back to Leyra's house. He glanced over his shoulder once to see Evander talking with the Betas on guard. He allowed himself to jog instead of walk, hoping to get away from Evander as soon as possible. It hurt his bruised legs, but he pushed through it.

It didn't take very long at all for him to run down the path and reach the other side of the trail, which opened up into the field holding the four big houses. Fox looked around, and he realized that this trail and the trail to the prison holes weren't too far apart from each other. This pack made sure that if they needed to move their lone wolves around, it wouldn't have to be far, and they wouldn't get a chance to see the territory or have time to escape.

Fox was a little relieved by the close proximity, though. If he ever did get moved to the bunkers and someone, maybe Seb, ever tried to hurt him, a loud enough commotion wouldn't go unnoticed by the Alphas. He was partially glad that Betas were posted at the bunkers, too.

Fox made his way across the field to Leyra's house. As he grew closer, he noticed Sunshine tending to a bed of wildflowers beside their backyard porch. He grew a little anxious at the sight of her, recalling her easy friendliness.

Sunshine straightened up and took off her gardening gloves, reaching beside her to grasp a bottle of water. She must've heard or smelled Fox coming, because she turned just enough to look behind her. She finished her sip of water and smiled at Fox. The gesture came so readily that Fox was momentarily stunned. After spending all day with Alpha Evander, meeting Sunshine's radiance was almost like experiencing emotional whiplash.

"Hello, Fox," she greeted, waving. Fox inclined his head a bit.

"Hello ma'am," he replied. He stepped carefully around Sunshine's garden, avoiding her beds of vegetables and arrangements of flowers. Fox looked around at her handiwork, her garden a mix of aesthetic flowers, vegetables, and berry bushes. There were stones arranged in small paths around her landscaping, partially overgrown with moss and clover. Fox took a deep breath in, a myriad of pleasant smells filling his lungs.

"You have a beautiful garden," he told her. She smiled wider. Fox was closer now, and her smile lessened a little as she took in the sight of his battered body. Fox avoided her gaze.

"Thank you. It's my pride and joy," she replied. Fox went over to the back porch and sat down on one of the steps, unsure if he was allowed to go inside on his own.

Sunshine was taking a look at her work in the backyard, probably trying to see it through a newcomer's eyes. She turned to him. "How was your day with Evander?" she asked. Fox pulled up his shoulders and tucked his hands under his legs.

"It was..." he searched for the right word. 'Good' would be a lie, 'okay' didn't feel right, and 'bad' was an overstatement. "It could've been worse," Fox admitted quietly, looking down at his shoes.

Sunshine hummed. "He's pretty hard on you lone wolves. But I think your manners will help keep him off your back for most of your time here. You behaved?"

Fox nodded. He was acutely aware of his bandaged shoulder and scratched chest and bruised limbs. It definitely could've been worse if he was the same as the other loners.

"Leyra is still out. You can hang out out here with me, if you'd like," Sunshine offered. Fox liked the comfort and relaxation her garden provided, so he nodded again.

For a while Sunshine worked, picking off dying leaves or ripping up weeds that could potentially kill her flowers, and pinching harmful bugs. Fox watched the sky as he noticed it began to sprinkle again.

"Does it rain a lot here?" he asked at one point.

Sunshine turned her gaze to the sky, smiling at the pileup of dark clouds. "It sure does. Snows a lot, too. I love the rain."

Fox only loved it when he wasn't caught in it, when he had a warm and securely covered shelter. But he enjoyed its smell and its sound, and when it was hot out, he enjoyed when it came and cooled him down.

A wave of nostalgia tried to bring certain memories back to the forefront of Fox's mind, but he shoved them away. He couldn't let that sadness take over him. Not until he was alone, at least.

He took a deep breath and sighed. It must've had a certain tone or air to it, because Sunshine looked at him. Fox avoided her gaze again.

"Do you know what it is I do here, besides garden?" she asked lightly. Fox shook his head. "I'm a therapist."

Fox became a little tense. "I've tried to offer therapy to the other lone wolves, but they don't trust me enough to let themselves be vulnerable around me. Or they simply don't want to dig up their past, or they don't want to get better. If you need to, you can talk to me. If you think it will help," Sunshine said.

Fox swallowed and fidgeted with his pants under his legs, picking at them. He had tried opening up to people before, but time and time again they proved to him that they didn't care, or they would use his past to take advantage of him. He had given up on talking about his past and his problems. He had learned that it was safer to keep everything to himself.

But Fox was also stuck here. He couldn't leave, and he wasn't sure if he'd ever get the nerve to try. He was still scared of these Alphas and what they could do to him. Fox was tired of pain, and wanted to avoid it as much as he could.

If he was going to spend a lot of time here, he might have to open up at some point. There were some things about him that the Alphas might need to know later on, or if he ever wanted to give friends a chance again, he'd have to talk. He'd have to talk about himself.

"Do you care?" Fox asked. He didn't ask it rudely, just genuinely. He wasn't going to waste his breath and his feelings if Sunshine was just fulfilling a job and not actually listening to help him.

"I care about every single one of my patients. Every person is an embodiment of a story, and stories deserve to be told, and they deserve to be heard. And with every story, you grow to care about the characters within them. Especially the main one," Sunshine said. She sat back on her heels and smoothed her skirt down her thighs, resting her palms there. "I care about stories an awful lot. I care about yours."

Fox raised his head to meet her eyes. She stared back, kindness and patience etched in every curve of her face. Her brown eyes were warm, and her hands looked gentle, and she exuded such calmness it almost unsettled Fox. Fox thought the little raindrops caught in the coils of her hair looked like glitter, or like stars in a night sky. Maybe she was an angel.

Another unexpected wave of nostalgia hit him. It was so strong that his breath stuttered and he felt the sting of tears under his eyes.

There had once been someone he could talk to all the time, about anything, about everything. The two of them would talk and listen in turn, give input or laugh or be astounded together. Fox had not talked to her in a long time, and he often wished he could.

He lifted a hand and pressed his wrist to his mouth, an effort to hide its brief tremble from Sunshine. But she could clearly see that Fox had been hit with an intense emotion, because her face softened even more.

"What are you feeling right now?" she asked sympathetically.

Fox's lips parted. He struggled to decide on whether he should say it. He wanted to. He really, really wanted to.

"I..." he looked at Sunshine. She seemed so readily open to accept what he was going to say. It wasn't often that someone was so willing to listen to him.

"Can I think about it? Your therapy," he asked.

Sunshine's visage briefly grew disappointed, but then morphed into understanding. "Of course," she responded. "I'll be here when you're ready. And that can be whenever, Fox. Whenever you need me."

Fox could only nod in response. He struggled to shove his rocky emotions back down under calm waters, but it helped that Sunshine didn't pressure him, and instead went back to tending her garden. The sprinkling rain turned a little more steady, but it wasn't enough to send them inside, so Fox focused on breathing in the damp smell of the earth and tried to stay present in the moment.

~Question: do you guys prefer longer chapters but updated less frequently, or do you prefer slightly shorter chapters that are updated more often?

Also I'm aware that numbing agents for stitches are usually topical creams rather than syringe fluid, but for the sake of hinting at Fox's backstory I used the latter

5, THE GOOD AND THE BAD OF MEALTIMES

Leyra arrived at the house about an hour later. She found the two of them still in the backyard. Fox tensed as the back door opened. He could feel the Alpha's skeptical eyes watching him. Sunshine stood and smiled at her mate, walking up the steps past Fox and placing a resounding kiss on Leyra's cheek.

"Hello my starling. How did your day go?" Sunshine greeted, her tone pleasant. Her demeanor had a quick impact on Leyra, because Fox could feel her heavy dominance ease off his back.

"Had to deal with some complaints, but other than that it wasn't too bad. How was yours?" Leyra replied. Fox was a little surprised at the lack of harshness in her tone. It was strange hearing Leyra speak more gently.

"It went quite well. I made progress in two of my sessions, and then I took care of some weeds and got rid of some pests out here. Fox kept me company for a little while, too, which was nice," Sunshine said. Fox's heart jumped at the mention of his name, but it calmed when Sunshine said his company had been nice.

"Really?" Leyra queried.

"Yes. He doesn't fill silence with idle chatter. It's nice to spend time with others without having to talk with them all the time," Sunshine told her.

"Well..." Leyra mused, sliding her arms around Sunshine's waist. "I'm glad you felt safe around him."

Fox could feel her gaze again. He chanced glancing up at her face, and was met with furrowed brows and pressed lips, but it wasn't an expression of judgment or dislike. More so, it seemed like she was trying to figure him out. The Alpha looked him over, taking in his bruises and bandages and ruined shirt.

"Is there anything you need me for, Alpha?" Fox asked politely. Leyra shrugged a shoulder, her expression changing into indifference.

"No, not for today. Dinner will be ready for the lone wolves in a couple hours, so you can rest here for a bit before heading to the bunkers," she told him. Fox nodded with a whispered thanks. He rose and followed the two werewolves inside.

The two headed into the kitchen to begin prepping their own dinner, and Fox headed over to the stairs. "Fox," Leyra called after him just before he left the kitchen.

He turned and met her gaze. "Yes, ma'am?"

"You'll probably be with Alpha Rishima or Alpha Ahren tomorrow, so if you need a new shirt, they can help you get one," she told him. Fox's eyebrows rose just a little, surprise catching him off guard. Maybe this was his reward for doing a good job cleaning up the concessions building?

The beginnings of a smile pulled at his mouth. "Thank you, Alpha," he replied, and she nodded at him before turning away.

Fox went upstairs. The more he thought about getting a brand new shirt, the wider his smile grew. By the time he reached his bedroom, he felt strangely giddy, like he'd just been given an unexpected gift. He almost couldn't believe it.

Fox whittled away his two hours of free time by checking on his belongings, and washing his bloodstained shirt in his bathroom sink. It took a while, but Fox was patient with the process, familiar with cleaning blood out of his clothes.

When that was done, he hung it up to dry over the shower railing and changed into a different shirt. The process had taken so long that by the time he finished pulling his shirt on, Leyra was at his door. "They're getting dinner ready for all of you, so start heading to the bunkers," she said.

Fox's stomach filled with dread as he imagined what it might be like having to eat around the other lone wolves, but he stood and went downstairs, with Leyra trailing behind him to make sure he went. He left out the back door and trudged across the field.

As he walked, he untied his jacket from around his waist and slipped it on. He wrapped it a bit tight around himself, and the pressure helped soothe his nerves a little.

He made his way out of the trees and into the bunker sector. There was already a Beta waiting at the end of the trail, and he glanced at Fox when he stepped out of the tree line. The Beta tilted his head to indicate for Fox to follow him, and the two of them walked around some of the bunkers to the big picnic bench in the center.

Fox couldn't help it, his shoulders tensed and his chest began to fill with little needles of anxiety, and his legs wanted to turn around and head back the other way. Fox swept his gaze over the lone wolves already seated. There were more men than women, some were older than him, most seemed to be the same age, only a couple looked younger.

He caught Seb's eye, who sat at one end of the table. Seb glowered at him, still not happy by the fact that Fox hadn't let him take the credit for his cleaning. Fox turned his gaze away, not interested in interacting with him.

"Sit here," the Beta leading him instructed. Fox was relieved to find he'd been seated at the opposite end of the table from Seb.

Fox took a seat. Nobody sat across from him, but a woman sat beside him. A good foot of space between them guaranteed some breathing room, which Fox was grateful for. He met eyes with the woman only briefly, enough to take in the bare minimum of her appearance. Blonde hair mishapenly cut around her shoulders, green eyes, skinny physique, white skin, slouched shoulders.

Fox looked around as discreetly as he could. He spotted four Betas but no Alphas, which gave him mixed feelings. He was glad Evander wasn't here, but he was also a little worried about how well four Betas could handle eleven lone loves. Well, ten, because Fox wasn't planning on fighting anybody.

The Beta who had led him to his seat took up post a few feet behind him. Fox wondered if he was there to observe Fox and his behavior when not in the presence of Alphas. Fox's legs began to grow jittery at the attention, hoping he wouldn't do anything to tarnish his image. He wanted to stay on the Alphas' good side for as long as he could.

He turned his head as he noticed movement to his left. Two more Betas emerged from the trees, pulling a big cart that carried two big jugs of water and three bins full of food. There were paper plates, paper cups, and disposable utensils, as well as a trash can.

At the sight and smell of the food, the other lone wolves shifted in their spots, agitated, hungry. The movement made Fox even more nervous.

The Betas pulling the cart stopped a safe distance away from the table, then began pulling out paper plates and scooping leftover food onto them. Fox counted; each plate got three scoops. The other Beta filled cups with water.

The two of them passed out the food. Fox and the woman next to him were given a plate first. Then the two next to the woman's other side were given their plates and cups, and so on down the table. The wolves at the other end were already baring their teeth and digging claws into the table, impatient.

The woman beside him didn't dig in right away, so neither did Fox. Fox realized, as he observed the other lone wolves, that the ones who seemed more disheveled or banged up were seated at one end, and others who were cleaner and didn't look like they'd been fighting were seated closer to his end.

"You may eat," the Beta behind him announced. Fox surveyed his food. There were bits of every kind of food, it seemed like. He spotted some overcooked rotini, some mushrooms, some smashed cherry tomatoes, a few carrot strings with dark spots, the hard ends of bread loaves that nobody seemed to like, a few bruised strawberries and blueberries, and potato skins.

They had been given the leftovers that nobody else had wanted. Fox wanted to ask about its origin, who had left all the food untouched, but was uncertain if he was allowed to. He side eyed the other lone wolves, who had immediately dug into their food. Some with more aggression than necessary, others a little more calmly.

Fox was used to eating less than ideal food. He may be curious about where all this came from, but it looked decent enough to eat, so he picked up a fork one of the Betas had set down by his plate and began to pick his serving apart.

He pushed aside the bits he didn't prefer, and took small bites of the stuff he did like. It was a strange mixture, so he separated everything as best he could.

Not too far into his meal, he felt eyes on him. He glanced out of the corner of his eye to the woman next to him. She was watching him like she had a question to ask.

"Hello," she greeted softly. She sounded close to the same age as Fox.

"Hi," Fox whispered back.

"I don't like tomatoes," she stated. Fox furrowed his brows a little, but after a glance at her plate, he understood. She had pushed her tomatoes in their own pile away from the rest of her portion. Fox had done the same with his mushrooms.

"I don't like mushrooms," he said, playing her game.

"Trade?" she offered. Fox nodded. The two of them pushed their plates closer together and they swapped the respective foods they wanted. Fox heard the Beta behind them step closer, watching what they were doing, but when it was obvious they weren't fighting over the food, he backed away.

"I'm Star," the woman said. Fox thought that name suited her, even though he knew nothing about her.

"I'm Fox." She smiled at his name rather than frowned, and Fox instantly warmed to her just for that response alone.

"It suits you," she observed. Fox liked her even more.

"Thanks. Yours too," he replied. She tucked her shoulders up, but kept smiling.

The two went back to eating. The hungrier wolves finished first, but the calmer ones spaced out their bites. Now that Fox had spoken to one of them, he felt more comfortable with observing the others. The woman who sat next to Star seemed to be older, there was a certain slouch in her back that hinted at general exhaustion. She had a shaved head of black hair and a few gnarly scars on her arms. The man across from Star also seemed quite a bit older, his brown hair beginning to gray on the sides, as well as in his short beard. He had a long scar spanning the side of his head and face, and the beginning of another on his collarbone, disappearing below his shirt. He looked like he once had a lot of muscle but had lost too much too fast.

They seemed to be minding their business, eyes on their food, but further down the table things were a bit more rowdy. Three werewolves were hunched protectively over their plates, scarfing everything down, and two others were staring Seb down for the remainder of his portion. Fox noticed the Betas moving closer, preparing to break up a fight. Fox also noticed that the werewolves seated around Seb had shock collars around their throats, too.

Seb bared his teeth at the two werewolves in front of him, growling as he clutched his plate. The werewolf next to Seb used the distraction as a chance to snatch a handful of what was left of Seb's food. Seb reacted instantly, whipping his head around to bite the other were-wolf's hand.

Fox watched his fangs sink deep into the thief's wrist. The thief was the same size as Seb, but had far paler skin and curly red hair, freckles dotting his face and arms. He yelped as Seb sank his teeth into his arm, but he stubbornly refused to let go of the food. He grabbed a fistful of Seb's hair with his free hand and started viciously yanking.

The Betas moved quickly, grabbing both werewolves by their necks and pinning them down against the table. One of them triggered the shock collar around both of their necks, and their faces twisted in pain, but they both still refused to let go.

Fox had seen on more than one occasion that when a werewolf had locked their jaws in a bite, the best way to pry them off to ensure minimal damage to the victim, was to choke them. The Betas seemed to know this, too.

The Betas struggled to pry Seb's teeth off of the redhead's arm, so one of them wrapped his arms around Seb's throat in a chokehold. The other Beta did the same with the redhead, who finally let go of the food to instead try and pull the Beta's arms away from his neck. Seb opened his jaw with a strangled gasp. He fought against the Beta, fists beating against the Beta's abdomen.

In the midst of the struggle, the other two werewolves who had been staring Seb's food down reached out to grab what was left. The rest of the Betas descended immediately.

Fox watched with a tense body and wide eyes as all the Betas wrestled the four lone wolves away from the table and began to drag them to their bunkers. The lone wolves fought them every step of the way, kicking and clawing and snarling profanities.

Seb was only dragged back just enough to stay out of reach of the redhead he'd been biting. When the redhead was dragged far enough away, the Beta growled in Seb's ear. "If you calm down, I'll get you a new portion, but if you go after Warren you're not getting anything."

Seb was still struggling against the Beta's grip, but at his offer, he stopped. He said something in a wheeze, and the Beta let him go.

He collapsed to his knees, gasping and coughing. The Beta stood behind him, waiting to see what he would do. Seb caught his breath. Fox could see him glaring daggers at Warren, the redhead, as he was being tossed into his bunker, but he didn't move to attack him. The Betas waited until Warren was locked inside.

"Okay. Sit down," the Beta behind Seb ordered. Seb complied, rubbing his throat. The Beta kept his promise and scooped a new portion of food onto a new plate, just enough to make up for what was lost, and gave it to Seb. Seb ate it in a hurry, probably not wanting to risk someone else trying to steal his food.

Fox released a stressed breath he didn't realize he'd been holding. He mused to himself that Seb was really not having a good day. He wondered if that was common for him.

Fox leaned a little closer to Star. "Does this happen at every meal-time?" he asked in a murmur. He could tell by the way she was running her hand up and down her forearm that the sudden fight had made her stressed, too.

"Not always. But sometimes," she answered quietly.

"If you're finished with your food, head back to your bunker," one of the Betas announced. Most of the occupants at the table had finished, so they stood and trudged back to their respective bunkers. Star had finished, too, so she stood and waved a little goodbye at Fox before walking away.

Fox was almost done. He ate the last few bites and tried to avoid eye contact with Seb. When he was done, he rose and threw his trash away, then began to walk back to the Alphas' houses. He could feel unfriendly eyes on him as he left, but he paid no mind to them.

When he made it back to Leyra's house, he knocked at the back door and waited. Sunshine answered it, letting him inside with a smile. As Fox entered the house, he saw Leyra lounging on the couch in pajamas and could smell popcorn in the kitchen. A movie was waiting to start playing on their big tv screen.

Fox rarely watched movies. If he ever saw a poster for a new one outside of a theater that piqued his interest, he would sneak inside to watch it, but Fox had only done that a few times in his life. Movies made him feel upset and frustrated. He always came out of them feeling like he wasted precious time, time he could've spent scavenging for food or scouting out new survival supplies, or traveling to one of his bucket list destinations. He spent the entire time watching movies feeling anxious and guilty at once, which made enjoying the movies difficult.

He passed through the living room and kitchen without another glance at the tv. He went upstairs and to his bathroom. He stripped and surveyed the extent of his wounds. The bruises would go away in a couple days. The claw marks on his chest would heal within the week. The bite wound on his shoulder, though, would take longer to seal and scar.

Fox took a long warm shower, basking in the steam. He took care in washing himself, and after his shower he cleaned around the stitches in his shoulder and chest, gritting his teeth at the sting and keeping his nose covered with a towel. He covered both areas with fresh gauze from a first aid kit he found in the cabinets under the sink, then went to his room.

The first thing he did was check his bag, making sure everything was still there and undisturbed. Leyra and Sunshine seemed to be keeping out of his space, though, which Fox was very grateful for. He wondered if that privilege was only given to him because he was docile and unthreatening. He was certain the other lone wolves had their things regularly searched.

Fox changed into the same pajamas he wore last night, and then he crawled into bed. It was just as comfortable as it had been last night, maybe even more so, the duvet a gentle weight against his exhausted body. Fox closed his eyes and listened to the quiet rain outside. There was no thunder or lightning tonight, but he slept just as soundly.

~~~

When Fox woke, he stayed in bed for as long as he was allowed to again. He stared at the window and the calm morning light and repeated in his head how grateful he was for everything he'd been given so far. He thanked the universe for this comfortable bed, for his few clothes, for his bag of belongings, for the food he was given, for the clean shower he had access to, and for the opportunity to relax for a few hours before having to start his day.
~~~

Around 9 in the morning this time, someone knocked on his door. It didn't quite sound the same as the knock he heard yesterday, and he detected Leyra's scent on the other side of the door.

Fox rose from the bed, grimacing at the ache in his limbs and chest. He reminded himself that he'd been through worse, and he'd need to tough it out until everything healed.

He opened the door and found Leyra already dressed. She gave him a once over in place of a greeting. "Get changed and freshened up. You'll be with Alpha Rishima today, but first you can grab breakfast with the other lone wolves."

"Yes ma'am," Fox murmured in reply. Leyra left to give him privacy. Fox sighed, wishing he could've had the same morning as yesterday, but Leyra had already told him not to expect that kind of treatment all the time.

Fox got changed into gray cargo pants and a black shirt. He took a peek outside his window to gauge the weather. The sky held less dark clouds than it did yesterday, and the sun was shining bright and warm on the world below. Fox tied his jacket around his waist again, though, just in case the afternoon or evening would bring more rain.

He freshened up in the bathroom, rinsing his face and brushing his teeth and checking to see if his hair was presentable. He messed with it a bit to make it appear less like he'd just woken up. When he was satisfied with his appearance, he cleaned his stitches again and applied fresh gauze.

Fox hid his bag in his closet, and then trotted downstairs. In the kitchen, Sunshine was enjoying a smoothie, and Leyra was nowhere to be found. Sunshine smiled in greeting. "Good morning, Fox."

Fox bowed his head a little. "Good morning. Can you tell me which house is Alpha Rishima's? I've been told I'm shadowing her today."

Sunshine nodded and set her smoothie down. She beckoned for Fox to follow her as she headed towards the front of the house. She pulled aside the curtains covering one of the front windows and pointed to a brown house with a brick walkway and patio. There were a few toys scattered on the front lawn, and the garage door was open, revealing more toys and bikes. Two cars were parked in the driveway.

"Right over there. She's the busiest of the four, not just because she runs the town affairs but also because she has four kids. If you're with her, she's probably going to keep you on your toes a lot," Sunshine said.

Fox started to grimace, but hid it away when Sunshine turned to him. "Off to breakfast?" she asked, her tone cheerful, even though she had to be aware of how tense mealtimes were for the lone wolves, and how subpar the food was.

"I am," Fox confirmed, and he reached for the front door. Sunshine bid him a good day, which Fox returned, and then he was off.

As he stepped outside, the morning warmth enveloped him. He took in a deep breath and sighed. Part of him wanted to go off and do his own thing, scavenge for firewood or hunt for food. He had gotten so used to living like that, to moving at his own pace, according to his own schedule, only submitting to the sun and how long it would stay in the sky. He hoped he would be allowed a day off to spend some time by himself. He didn't really want to be catering to the Alphas every single day.

He made a mental note to ask Rishima about that.

He set off towards the bunkers. Just as he arrived there, the other lone wolves were emerging from their bunkers and taking seats at the picnic table. Six Betas already stood around it, two at the same food cart as last night and one at each corner of the table.

Fox took a seat at the same spot he'd sat at last night. He kept his head tilted down and his hands folded in his lap, but he secretly watched the other loners as they took their seats. Fox noticed that this time, there didn't seem to be an apparent order in which everyone sat. Disgruntled faces mixed with tired faces.

Someone sat down next to Fox. He looked over and found Star there. She smiled at him, waving in a silent greeting, and Fox smiled a little in return. An anxious twist in his chest unwound when he saw that a friendly face had sat next to him.

But a moment later, it twisted tight again when he saw that Seb sat down across from him. Fox's brows furrowed in a displeased frown, but he didn't look at Seb.

Seb kicked his foot under the table. "So where are you staying, if it's not in a bunker?" he bluntly asked. His tone was already bordering on hostile, either because he was still unhappy about yesterday, or he was unhappy about the fact that Fox had gotten to sleep elsewhere. Maybe it was both, stacked on top of each other to create a pile of general dislike.

Seb asked his question just loud enough to catch the attention of a few other lone wolves at the table. Fox pretended not to notice. He leveled a look at Seb. "In one of the holes," he lied.

Seb narrowed his eyes. For werewolves, detecting lies was based entirely on skill, on being able to read body language so well you knew what was true and what was fake. Alphas were trained to have this skill. Betas were also adept at deciphering truth from lie, although they could still have some difficulty. Regular pack wolves struggled more. Lone wolves learned this skill through bad encounters with each other.

Fox could pick up on lies in an instant. He wasn't sure if Seb held the same level of skill.

Fox watched as Seb's eyes flitted over Fox's face and upper body. Fox did his best to appear bored and not nervous, keeping his shoulders relaxed and his expression blank.

"You don't look like you've been sleeping in a hole," Seb observed.

"I took a shower before I came here," Fox stated. Seb's eyes narrowed again, his lips pressing together.

"Where?" he pressed.

"Who cares, Seb?" Star interjected.

Seb bared his teeth at her. "I care, and so should every one of us, because this sack of fresh meat is living better than the rest of us, and I want to know why."

"I'm not living better than the rest of you," Fox retorted, feeling figurative hackles rising on the back of his neck. Fox might've been dealt a good hand for his time here at Lily of the Valley Pack, but Fox had lived a life as difficult and painful as any other lone wolf. Perhaps more so, if Fox dared to bring up memories of darker times with the scientists who had experimented on him.

"I saw you heading to the Alphas' houses last night. You're living large with one of them, aren't you?" Seb accused. His brows were furrowed in a glare, and his teeth were growing sharper.

Fox could feel Star's gaze on the side of his head. He didn't want to lose a potential friend just because he'd been placed with an Alpha for the time being. Fox exhaled sharply through his nose.

"There's no room for me here right now, so they're letting me stay at one of their houses. But the moment I slip up, I'm stuck sleeping outside in the rain. And the moment one of you dies, I'm moving into your bunker. I'm not living large. I've kept my head down enough for the Alphas to give me their spare room, but they're watching me like hawks," Fox admitted.

He hated outing himself, hated revealing that he had a room instead of a hole in the ground. But maybe admitting this to Seb and Star, and the rest of the table that was surely listening in now, Fox could decipher who was a true ally and who was a true threat. Chances were, Fox had just made enemies with everyone here. But Fox hadn't been expecting anything different.

"Did you fool them? Or are you truly a good person?" Star asked him. Fox was suddenly aware that the Betas were listening, too. He could feel their curious gazes, and their lack of interference up to this point hinted that they were gathering more information on him.

Fox exhaled soundly again, though this time it was less temperamental and more mildly exasperated. "I'm just trying to get by with the least amount of pain possible. Alphas will treat you better if you respect them. That's all I'm doing. Respecting them so that they won't hurt me."

"Smart," someone else at the table said. Fox looked over to see the scarred older lone wolf with graying hair had spoken. "Some of us still haven't figured that out." He gave a pointed look at Seb. Seb met it with a glare.

"Some of them are still assholes even if you do follow orders," he retorted.

"Enough," one of the Betas barked. "Settle down or your portions will be two scoops instead of three."

Everyone quieted down. Seb crossed his arms in petulance, scowling at Fox. Fox held his gaze, a silent gesture of defiance. Seb didn't like him, he didn't like Seb. Fox wanted to avoid fighting as much as possible, but he also didn't want Seb to think he was timid enough to be pushed around.

The Betas portioned out their breakfast and set everything down in front of the lone wolves. This morning, their meal consisted of leftover undercooked waffles, blueberry pancakes, chopped fruit that was a little slimy and bruised, and scraps of eggs varying in texture. It was better than last night's meal, and the lone wolves, including Fox, dug in and ate every last morsel. Fox and Star didn't trade anything, but neither of them had anything they wanted to trade.

Cups of water were emptied and plates were scraped clean. When everyone was finished, the Betas had everyone throw their trash away and line up to be given orders on where to go for their labor. Fox listened in, even though he already knew where he was going. Some of the lone wolves were sent to Evander to assist with more recruit training. Some were sent to town to help with a construction project. A couple were sent to what a Beta called the 'waste sector', and Fox wasn't sure if that meant general trash or excrement. He didn't want to find out. Star and a couple others were sent to the farm sector.

A Beta told Fox where to go, even though Fox already knew, but he didn't say as much and simply trekked back through the trees to the Alphas' houses.

He made his way over to the house with a bunch of toys scattered on the lawn, and found that the garage door was still open. Fox slowed to a stop at the end of the driveway, uncertain about how to proceed. Should he walk up to the front door or the inside garage door? Should he take advantage of this chance to have a little more time to himself and wait until someone comes outside?

Fox remembered Evander's harshness yesterday, the way he still treated Fox like any other lone wolf even though Fox hadn't yet acted like every other lone wolf. Evander was searching for any hint that Fox was an unreliable and ill-natured person, prone to violence and bad temper. Fox liked to think that he was none of those things, that he was cautious rather than unreliable, level-headed rather than ill-natured, self-preserving rather than violent. But Fox knew that every lone wolf held those traits, too, but they grew worse over time, feeding the stereotypes and proving the pack wolves right. Fox didn't want to become another terrible loner. He wanted to be viewed as someone different in a good way. He wanted to look out for himself and ensure a decent life here.

In order to do that, he needed to be on his best behavior, and he needed to make good decisions. A good decision would be to knock on the front door and wait for someone to answer it. A bad decision that would surely catch Evander's attention would be to loiter out in the street.

Fox approached the front door and knocked. As he waited, he could hear commotion inside the house, feet thumping in quick fashion on hardwood floors, a door slamming shut, someone reprimanding the door slam, a little kid screaming, an older kid's voice asking where her shoes are, someone else yelling that they saw them by the front closet, and the older kid replying that they weren't there, and so on. After a minute of no one answering the door, Fox considered the doorbell. It was louder and announced his presence more directly, something that made him uncomfortable. He decided against it and knocked again.

More commotion, no answer. Fox sighed and scanned the front yard. On their brick patio, they had some cushioned outdoor chairs and a table. Fox sat down in one of the chairs and waited.

He was a little glad no one had answered the door to let him in. He didn't really want to be caught up in the chaos ensuing inside the house. This gave him a chance to have more time to himself, too, and if Evander spotted him, or anyone else for that matter, he could say that he knocked twice already with no answer, and it wouldn't be a lie.

Fox let his gaze roam as he waited. He gathered some finer details on his surroundings, like moss growing between the bricks in Rishima's yard, and a few homemade bird houses hung up in the trees in the Alphas' front yards, where robins and chickadees flitted in and out. A calm breeze had picked up since his trek from the bunkers, which left him wondering if the wind would worsen and bring rain clouds with it.

Movement caught his eye. The other male Alpha he hadn't yet officially met was emerging from the blue house that had the outdoor heaters and swimming pool. He locked his front door with a set of keys and ambled down his front porch steps, taking his time.

The Alpha swept his gaze over the trees and the other houses. He seemed to just be taking in the view, but the muscles in Fox's back wound tight when the Alpha's gaze halted on him. Fox wanted to look down, avoid eye contact even from this far away, but a survivalist impulse made him watch the potential threat.

The Alpha, Ahren, seemed to glance around Rishima's house, then returned his gaze to Fox. Fox wondered if he was going to get in trouble, either for waiting out here or for sitting on furniture that wasn't his. But even despite his growing anxiety, he stayed put. Maybe he was stuck in a freeze response.

Ahren started walking over to him. Fox's breath caught as a bolt of panic shot through his chest, a painful sensation, and he gripped his thighs tightly to balance it out. He couldn't take his eyes off the Alpha as he approached.

Ahren moved just as leisurely as he had when he emerged from his house. He wore brown outdoor pants similar to Fox's, and a regular gray shirt. He had full brown hair grown out just enough to cover his forehead and curl around his ears, and his skin was incredibly suntanned, more than anyone Fox had seen so far. As he grew closer, he cataloged a few patchwork tattoos on his forearms, as well as the same amount of scarring as the rest of the Alphas, and the same amount of musculature. He seemed a bit more lean than Evander, though, but roughly the same height, give or take a couple inches.

Fox watched as Ahren walked up the brick path to the patio. He didn't take his eyes off Fox, probably gathering the same information that Fox was obtaining on him. Ahren finally moved his gaze away to stare at the front door, listening to the noise inside the house.

A smile graced his face, and he turned a pair of dark brown eyes on Fox. "How long have you been waiting?" he asked.

Fox drew his shoulders up with a nervous glance at the door. "A few minutes, I think, sir. Maybe ten."

Ahren's smile widened a little more when Fox said 'sir'. He considered the door again, then swept his gaze over the area again. "How about you come with me for now. Rishima is probably going to be a while, and I can send you over when she needs you later."

Fox hadn't been expecting this. Ahren seemed a thousand times calmer than Rishima's house, though, and he had a feeling he might fare better with him than with her. "Okay," was all he said.

He stood, and Ahren began to lead him to some unknown destination.

6, ALPHA AHREN

The two of them walked down the dirt road. Fox kept a comfortable distance away from Ahren, trailing behind him. Not long into the walk, though, Ahren looked over his shoulder at Fox with a certain expression on his face, and Fox got the inclination that Ahren didn't like him being at his back. Fox moved to the side a bit so he was somewhat in step with the Alpha, but not directly next to him.

"I see Evander was none too gentle with you yesterday," Ahren noted. Fox still ached from yesterday, but he was doing his best to ignore his bruises and shoulder.

He was uncertain how to respond. It was an open-ended statement, inviting response but not requiring it. Fox wanted to tell him that he'd behaved as best he could, but Evander had put him in his place anyway. He didn't know if Ahren would believe him if he tried defending himself.

He decided to give it a shot. "I didn't understand why he let his recruits fight me. I did what he asked and cleaned the little snack shack, and I told him the truth when Seb tried to lie about who did what. Later, he told me it was just because I am a lone wolf, and no matter what good I do, I'm still going to be treated like one."

As Ahren listened, he nodded once and his expression turned partially understanding and partially disappointed. "We have to be hard on all of you, regardless of how well you do. If we don't maintain dominance, then you loners will start to give yourselves privileges," he explained.

Fox frowned. "Why are we not allowed any privileges?"

Ahren looked at him. "You'll get some privileges, of course. But you won't get enough to become a genuine member of the pack."

Fox could feel the beginnings of frustration brewing in his chest. It was mainly directed at the unspoken rule every single pack seemed to follow; lone wolves weren't allowed to be accepted in. "Why are we not allowed to become true members?"

"Too many of you let your problems affect others around you. In your grief or your anger, in your trauma, you more often than not end up hurting people. And some of you choose darker paths in life that destroy other lives. It's safer to turn you all away rather than take a chance," Ahren answered.

"Then why keep us here at all? Why not turn us away like every other pack?" Fox asked. He didn't realize how hungry he was for the answer.

Ahren took a deep breath. Fox was uncertain if it was a sign of impatience or irritation. He watched the Alpha closely, but all Ahren did was look up at the trees they passed under, expression still calm, his gate still relaxed.

"Safety, mostly. If we let you go, then there's a chance you could spill information about our pack to other lone wolves, and if enough of you hear about what we have to offer, then you might band together to try and attack us. If we keep you here after your first trespass, then there's no chance of that happening. Rumors will spread that lone wolves who enter here don't ever leave, which will then deter other lone wolves from coming close, and the threat of an attack lessens. Granted, it's equally dangerous to keep you inside the territory, close to the pack, but a threat that we know about is easier to manage than a threat we don't know about. Is all this making sense?" Ahren explained.

Fox was surprised by such a thorough answer. But it did make sense. Lily of the Valley Pack was widely known for being self-sustainable and accommodating to all its members, but the specific details of the pack were mysteries. Even letting outside loners know about where the barracks for the patrol wolves was located could be enough to blow open a weak spot in the territory, making the pack more vulnerable. Even though Lily of the Valley Pack was the largest pack around, a well-planned attack from a smaller group could still lead to catastrophe.

"I understand," Fox replied.

Ahren smiled a little. Fox settled down in his barrage of questions, and the two of them walked quietly to wherever Ahren was taking them. Fox took mental notes on where they went, taking in landmarks and how long it took to walk to certain spots. They walked down the dirt road that led to town, but then they veered off the road and into the woods, taking yet another worn path through the foliage.

At some point during their walk, Ahren struck up conversation again.

"Fox is a very uncommon name," he mused. "Did your father or your mother name you?"

Fox caught on to the way Ahren phrased that question. It was like a little hook in his head, tugging just gently enough to draw his attention. He peered at the Alpha. Fox could lie, but Ahren could catch on to that and it would not leave a good first impression. Fox didn't want both male Alphas to dislike him, so he decided against lying.

He wasn't willing to reveal too much about himself just yet. Fox knew if he revealed that he had named himself, then Ahren would press for his old name. Fox's younger self, before he truly became a lone wolf, had died a long time ago, and Fox wanted his birth-given name to remain dead with him. He didn't trust strangers to respect his wishes on being called Fox instead of his dead name, so he wasn't going to reveal that tidbit about him at all.

"I would rather not talk about my parents," Fox murmured, dodging the question entirely and shutting down any further questions about his past.

"Touchy subject?" Ahren queried.

"Partially. Yes," Fox replied. He held little regard for his father, who'd been absent for a majority of his life, but his mother... Just the thought of her made his chest tighten painfully, and he shoved away the memories that threatened to surface.

"My apologies," Ahren said. Fox glanced at him again. He wasn't sure if Ahren was going to be the same as Leyra, only barely caring about the fact that he had jabbed a wound that hadn't yet healed.

"So... did you really trespass on accident?" Ahren asked next.

"I did. I was hitchhiking and the route the driver took brought me into your land," Fox stated. In retrospect, Fox wished he had known this pack's location beforehand, so he could avoid the area entirely. He kind of wished he hadn't hitchhiked, either, because on foot he would've been able to smell the pack long before coming close to its border.

"Hm..." the Alpha hummed. He didn't sound convinced, just like Leyra. Fox couldn't help letting an annoyed and tired sigh escape his lungs. Ahren glanced at him, but Fox kept his gaze on his feet. He didn't want to keep talking about himself or his mistakes, so he changed the subject.

"Can I ask what we're doing today?" he prompted.

"We're going to take a look at the campsite and see if it needs cleaning up," Ahren said. Fox tilted his head. Campsite?

Ahren seemed to read the confusion on Fox's face. "Part of my job is to help the pack maintain peace between their wild nature and their domesticated nature. Each werewolf has a conventional home, with all the modern amenities they need, but too much time spent indulging human needs can neglect our wild needs. So we have a campsite, a designated area for primitive camping, living without luxury items and accommodating our wolf nature. Leyra assists with this too, she organizes hunt rotations so that everyone in the pack has a chance to hunt as a wolf on a regular basis."

"Oh. I see," Fox replied. He thought it was smart of them to have a system like that, to ensure equilibrium within each of their members. "What about pups who aren't old enough to hunt?"

"We have a few safe areas for them to play as wolves," Ahren answered. For some reason, mentioning the pups made Fox think of his own time as a pup. He hadn't played with other werewolves. He had usually played by himself.

He wanted to ask more questions about the pack, but Fox had a feeling that if he pried too much, the Alphas would grow suspicious and think he was up to something. Fox was only out to protect himself, and nothing more, so he kept quiet.

Ahren didn't comment on anything else. They continued to traverse through the forest until they came across a wider path, and a wooden signpost that read "Campsite." Fox took in the mixture of giant trees that provided a wide-reaching canopy, and the smaller trees that provided coverage for the forest floor. Shrubs and ferns brushed against their ankles. The dirt was cool and spongy under their feet.

"We're just checking for any remnants of trash that shouldn't be here, and excrement that nobody buried or picked up and threw away. We try to enforce a leave-no-trace rule, but not everyone follows it, especially when they think no one is going to make them face any consequences," Ahren said.

"How are you able to tell who didn't follow the rule?" Fox asked.

"It'll be disgusting, but we'll sniff the feces and track down the person that way." Fox pulled a face, which Ahren saw. "Embarrassing on both ends, I know, but it's more embarrassing for the rule-breaker."

Ahren led Fox over to a wooden billboard that had a map of the surrounding campsite, and a small metal trash can with free poop bags in its own compartment on top. Ahren grabbed a few and handed them to Fox, then took a few for himself.

"See this map here?" Ahren said, pointing to a red spot on an obvious pathway. "This is where we are now. We'll start from the left side and work our way up and around to the right side, then circle back here."

"Yes, sir," Fox acknowledged. He took a moment to study the map, and found that it covered quite a bit of land.

The two of them began scouring the forest floor for trash and feces. Fox wondered why there would be trash if this campsite was for the bare minimum primitive kind of camping, but maybe there were people who didn't follow that rule, either.

He kept within sight of Ahren, so Ahren wouldn't have to be concerned of Fox deliberately wandering off. Over the course of two hours, they gradually picked their way through underbrush, trees, decaying logs, streams, and boulders.

They found someone's stash of garbage strewn around a makeshift fireplace. Fox studied the fire pit and narrowed his eyes in distaste at how poorly-made it was. He held further disdain for the chip bags and marshmallow sticks left behind.

"If they don't use the campsite the way they're supposed to," Fox asked as they picked up the garbage, "doesn't it damage their wild side? Because they're not satisfying it correctly?"

"It does exactly that," Ahren replied with an astonishingly proud smile directed at Fox, so obviously pleased that Fox momentarily froze in his movement. He did a double-take, but the Alpha was already turning away to pick apart the sad fire pit. "So many werewolves get too used to a pampered modern life and choose not to live in equality with nature. They're only harming themselves in the long run, and in the end they'll only have themselves to blame."

For some reason, this made Fox think about the different lone wolves he'd encountered over the years. Some had become loners through tragedy, either a pack falling apart or a family falling victim to some danger or another, or by losing a mate and going mad with heartbreak. Others had become loners by choice, either because their pack treated them terribly or they felt that their life paths led elsewhere.

Some were simply evil at heart, hurting others because they enjoyed it or because it brought them profit, and their sinister ways eventually had them cast out from their pack, if they weren't killed beforehand.

But Ahren's statement had Fox wondering if there were other ways that pack wolves became lone wolves. "Do..." he started to ask, but he suddenly felt self-conscious about asking so directly. He stammered for a moment, to the point the Alpha turned a patient look on him, and he simply scrapped his current thought and started over. "I have a question." That seemed more respectful.

Ahren smiled, vaguely amused. "Yes?"

"If they neglect their wolf nature, do they... deteriorate? Mentally or physically? Enough to... enough to become..." Fox was still struggling with directly asking him.

Ahren's expression grew more solemn. "Yes. Both, actually. When their equilibrium is too disrupted it can sometimes get to an irreversible point, and they start to go crazy. It's only downhill from there."

Fox hesitated. The Alpha seemed to sense the apprehension within Fox, and he approached him. Fox tensed and kept his gaze on his feet. Ahren got close enough that he could feel his dominant atmosphere envelope him. "Just ask, Fox. I won't be upset by curiosity."

Fox swallowed. "Do they become lone wolves?"

Ahren sighed. "They do."

Fox took a couple steps back, needing to separate himself from Ahren's intense scent and aura. "Do you cast them out?"

"We have to," Ahren replied. "They become a danger to the pack, and there's nothing we can do to help them."

"So you'll force lone wolves who trespass to stay, but you'll cast out your own members?" Fox asked. He felt a sting of unfairness.

"If a lone wolf that trespasses is crazy enough that they're a danger to others, we kill them. We know our pack, though, and killing them would take a toll on everyone, so we cast them out," Ahren said.

"But some of the lone wolves you keep are still dangerous even without being crazy—"

"I know," Ahren interrupted. Fox drew his shoulders up and kept his gaze respectfully downward. "That's why we continuously put them in their place, and if they fuck up enough times, we kill them."

Fox had almost forgotten about that. He wrapped his arms around himself and turned away, further performing submissive body language. "But the ones you cast out, you just let them go crazy all alone? Dissolve into madness in the wilderness?" he asked quietly.

Ahren must have noticed a certain tone to Fox's voice, because his next words were also soft. "We can't help them. Believe me, if we could, we would."

That statement reminded Fox, with another unfair sting, that pack wolves cared for each other in a way that Fox would never understand.

Fox's breath caught, and he readjusted his trash bag to distract Ahren. The Alpha took a moment to study him, though, but Fox looked everywhere but his direction. Eventually, the Alpha kicked some dirt over the burnt remnants of the fire, and continued walking. Fox followed him.

They cleared the left side of the campsite over the next hour. As they came around the back to the right side, they came across the very thing Fox was hoping to avoid.

"Ah... here we go," Ahren said with an air of long-suffering resignation. Fox grimaced as the Alpha crouched down and used a poop bag to scoop up a pile of werewolf feces that had been poorly buried by some foliage.

Ahren straightened, holding the pile up. "Honestly, the worst part about my job, aside from what we just discussed."

Fox watched with a scrunched nose as the Alpha brought the pile close to his face and gathered a deep inhale. Ahren let a good lungful in before he scrunched up his own nose and snorted, shaking his head in a very animalian way. He tied up the bag, sealing the poop away.

He met eyes with Fox, both of them sharing their silent disgust with each other. "Well, we're going to have to make a pit stop after this."

"You know whose it is?" Fox queried. Ahren nodded.

"This isn't the first time they've shat here and didn't take care of it," he said, clearly miffed by the transgression. "Next time we need a cleanup, I'm making him do it."

Fox was a little glad to hear that there was some sort of disciplinary system in place for their own pack members, too.

They finished up in the campsite, only coming across one other site with plastic trash. When they were done, they tossed the garbage into the trash can by the map billboard, and Ahren held on to the poop bag as they began walking back the way they had come earlier.

"After I take care of this, I'll give you a tour of my other sectors," Ahren told Fox. He nodded his acknowledgment and dutifully followed the Alpha.

Ahren took him through the forest and onto a paved road. They walked alongside said road for about half an hour, until they reached a suburban housing section, mostly filled with townhomes. There were flowery shrubs and tall oak trees lining lawns and curbs, providing a cozy and homely vibe to the area. Fox imagined how pretty it must be in autumn.

As they walked, Fox took in the sight of the townhomes. Each one seemed to have a similar layout, but each one also had its own character. Many houses were painted in fun uncommon colors, or had gardens like Sunshine's, or toys strewn on the front yard like Rishima's, or had porch swings with outdoor decorations lining small patios, or had enclosures for pets like chickens and rabbits. There was even a cat lounging on top of a mailbox, who chirped a greeting at them as they passed. Ahren reached up and petted the cat, receiving a pleased purr in response. Fox kept his hands to himself, just in case.

Ahren turned into a walkway that led up to a green townhouse. Fox let himself fall a little behind in step, and watched as the Alpha strode up to the front door and knocked. It was a demanding and resounding sound, and Fox felt the hairs on the back of his neck stand on end. Maybe Ahren was more upset by this than he was showing in his body language.

The door opened, and a woman appeared in the frame. Fox came to a stop halfway up the walkway.

"I'd like to speak with your mate," Ahren stated, not bothering to beat around the bush.

The woman briefly glanced at Fox, but nodded wordlessly and disappeared inside the house. A few moments later, a man took her place.

"Hello, Alpha Ahren. What's the issue?" he greeted, completely unperturbed by the visit. Fox swallowed as he noticed Ahren's shoulders tighten at the back.

He held up the bag of feces. "This is the issue, Phillip. Your shit."

Phillip's face paled, and he averted his gaze away. "Oh, I- I thought I buried it, like you said we could do. We can bury them, right? Did the rules change?" he stammered.

"Yes you can bury them. At least, and I mean minimum, six inches underground. Ideally, ten inches. Even better is to just scoop this up yourself and toss it," Ahren replied. Fox silently inched away, slowly making his way back down the walkway to the sidewalk by the road. Phillip made a series of uncertain sounds, trying to come up with words to defend himself.

"This is strike three, Phillip. Next week's cleanup is on you," Ahren said. "And after that, you can clean the public bathrooms by the pup playground."

Phillip stiffened in indignation. "The bathrooms too? Sir, I swear I'll clean up after myself better next time."

"I've heard this excuse a dozen times at this point. You and your mate need to quit bringing packaged snacks and quit shitting in the woods and leaving it behind for other people to clean up. Hiding it under some leaves isn't doing anything. Do you know why we have to bury our feces? If our shit gets into the wildlife's systems, it's going to affect their health, which will affect our food, and could potentially circle back around and get our pack members sick. Do you want to be responsible for a possible pack-wide illness?" Ahren continued. He wasn't going easy on Phillip, and his heated tone made Fox so wary he turned and hurried to the sidewalk, seeking to hide behind one of the shrubs that lined the curb.

"No, Alpha, I- I— Do you realize your loner is trying to sneak away right now?" Phillip countered. Fox froze.

Ahren turned and found Fox wide eyed and tense, arms tucked against his stomach. He took in the space between them, but Ahren hadn't originally known how far back Fox had kept from him to begin with. Phillip pointed an accusing finger at him.

"Yeah, he was just sneaking away towards the street," Phillip continued, and Fox recognized what he was doing. Shifting the Alpha's attention from him to Fox, and laying new blame on a lone wolf to distract from his own transgression, and to get Fox into trouble in hopes of Ahren forgetting about his anger towards Phillip.

Fox met Ahren's gaze. It wasn't challenging, just imploring. Ahren had narrowed eyes, but the set of his eyebrows and mouth told Fox that he was pondering him, not yet angry. Fox didn't know what to do. He turned his gaze down and crouched down onto the pavement, resting on his heels and hugging his knees to his chest.

"No, don't play innocent, I just saw you!" Phillip accused. Fox merely stayed as he was.

"Enough, Phillip. He's not going anywhere now, and I'll deal with him in a moment. But as for you, you can certainly highlight next Thursday in your calendar for cleanup of both the campsite and the playground bathrooms. If I catch you leaving shit out in the woods, regardless of what kind, you're going to be on cleanup duty for the rest of the year. Am I clear?" Ahren said.

Phillip fidgeted in his spot, glancing between Fox and Ahren. Eventually, he replied with a resigned "Yes, Alpha."

"Good." Ahren tossed the bag of poop onto the pavement in front of Phillip's front door, and without another word, he turned and headed back down the walkway. Fox felt a bolt of painful panic shoot through his chest at the Alpha's approach, and hid his face in his knees.

The Alpha came to a stop in front of him. He was silent for a moment, and Fox continued to hide in the only way available right then. Anxiety slowly seeped into his muscles, though, making each breath gradually feel more and more like needles in his lungs.

"I want you to be completely honest with me, Fox. Did you or did you not just try and sneak away to run?" Ahren asked.

Fox swallowed. He swallowed again. He drew in a stuttering and sharp breath. "No, Alpha," he answered. He swallowed once more and gathered the strength to lift his head up to peer at the Alpha. "No, Alpha," he repeated.

Ahren was looking down at him with that same unconvinced but thoughtful expression. "What were you doing?"

"I..." Fox licked his quickly drying lips, "I didn't realize how-" he paused to suck in a breath, "how upset you were, and I just wanted to-" he sucked in another breath, "to put distance between us. Just distance, I promise, Alpha."

To Fox's great relief, Ahren's expression melted into sympathy. Maybe it was because of how obvious Fox's anxiety was, how nervous Ahren's potential anger was making him. "Distance?" he repeated, but he didn't sound like he didn't believe Fox. Fox nodded quickly, hiding his face in his knees again.

Fox gasped as he felt a hand ruffle his hair. "I see. I appreciate your honesty."

Fox was momentarily stunned, both by the gesture and his words. He had a feeling that if Evander had been here instead of Ahren, Fox wouldn't have gotten off so easily.

"I think Leyra said you were supposed to get some new clothes today," Ahren stated, and Fox's heart leapt at the word clothes, plural. Would he get more than just a shirt?

Fox looked up at him, surprised and needing to see if Ahren was being serious. The Alpha smiled at him. He waved at Fox to stand. "Come on then. We'll do your tour first, and then clothes after."

"Thank you, Alpha," Fox replied, and forced himself to stand despite the fact that his legs were still ridding themselves of his anxiety's effects.

Fox glanced back at an open-mouthed Phillip, who still stood by his front door and had watched the whole exchange. Ahren ignored him, however, and began walking to the road. Fox followed.

"Well as you've seen already, this section here is where the pack members live. Bigger families live in houses, and single or double occupants live in townhouses like these," Ahren explained as they walked down the road.

Ahren didn't seem so upset anymore, so Fox didn't feel a need to keep his distance. He kept at Ahren's side but not directly next to him, like he had earlier in the day. Walking helped the rest of his muscles unwind, and soon the needles in his chest were gone.

Ahren took him to the pup playground he had mentioned to Phillip. It wasn't very far from the housing sector, but it was just far enough that it was surrounded by a decent amount of forest and required a quick trip down a small dirt trail. The playground itself consisted of two large separate jungle gyms, both connected by one long row of monkey bars. In one section of the park, there were swings, in another there was a sand pit with the type of sand you would find at a seaside beach, and in another spot were horizontal spinning wheels you could sit on and have someone else spin you around in circles, and in another area was maze of boulders and rocks that created small alcoves and caves. In its own little area were two picnic benches covered by a wooden roof, and the public bathrooms Ahren had mentioned before, as well as a small field that Fox could only guess was used for the pups to run around and play tag or play-hunt.

Fox could tell the pups here were well entertained. He himself would've had a blast here when he was younger. He probably would have come here every day. He tried not to feel jealous of the fact that he hadn't gotten to play in a park like this when he was younger.

After showing him the playground, Ahren took Fox to a large field he called the bonding sector. Fox thought he meant it was for mate bonding, but Ahren was quick to explain that this large field was dedicated to events that all pack members were invited to, every Friday and Saturday night. They sometimes held dance parties, or outdoor movie nights, or adults-only nights, or mates-only nights, or festive get-togethers around holidays and other significant days of the year. Ahren tried his best to keep the events fresh and regularly circulated, so that the pack wouldn't get bored of the same thing every weekend.

"For Halloween, we turn this into a haunted 'house', among other fun festive activities for all ages," Ahren put his fingers up in mock quotation marks for 'house'. Halloween wasn't for another couple of months, but it was the closest upcoming holiday that Fox knew would be excitedly celebrated by the pack. Fox, once again, tried his best not to feel jealous at the fact that he hadn't gotten to experience celebrating Halloween with a pack. He hoped, at least a little, that he might get to have a small share in that experience this year. If things didn't go south for him before then.

Aside from a snack shack similar to the one in the training sector, there wasn't much to see in the way of the bonding sector, so off they went again without further ado. "That's mostly everything for my specific sections. There's also an office down at the town hall building where pack members can leave complaints, suggestions, or reviews for me to consider. A few Betas help me with event planning and maintenance of my sectors. You'll probably help with cleanup most of the time, or since you're docile, you can help run some stands during events," the Alpha said.

Fox wasn't sure how he felt about potentially being amidst so many werewolves during those events. A trickle of anxiety slipped through his veins at the thought. He didn't comment on it, though, he just nodded to show the Alpha he understood and was willing to obey whatever he was directed to do.

Fox hadn't asked many questions, or even talked that much at all, since their visit to Phillip's house. The two of them were walking along the road towards town now, presumably to get Fox his new clothes, and Ahren studied Fox's profile.

"You've grown awfully quiet again. Like how you were in the prison hole," Ahren noted. His voice held a gentle invitation to it, something that Fox picked up on, but was confused by. He frowned a little. He tried to think of a response, but came up with nothing, so he merely shrugged his shoulders.

"Do you think I'm still upset?" Ahren asked him. Fox tucked his jacket around himself and shrugged again.

"I... with all due respect, sometimes I don't need to talk," Fox said. He added the beginning part in when he thought his statement might come off as rude. He thought about when Sunshine had mentioned how it was nice that Fox hadn't filled space with unnecessary talking.

"That's fair," Ahren replied, and he fell quiet. The two of them continued to walk in silence, listening to the wind rustle the tree leaves around them. Fox puzzled over why Ahren had picked up on his silence, why he worried if Fox thought he was still upset, or if he was even truly worried at all and was simply trying to figure him out, the same way Leyra tried to figure him out sometimes.

Fox was used to not talking for long periods of time. He'd gone weeks without uttering a word before, and more than a few times. He knew he could be quiet, but whenever he found himself in company with relatively friendly lone wolves, he exchanged unimportant conversation easily. He supposed he didn't really talk unless he needed to, or if he just had some questions.

Fox hoped that the Alphas would appreciate that. But he worried that the Alphas might be suspicious of him for his silence. He really didn't want to, but if he had to dredge up his past for the sake of gaining their favor, he'd try his best to do it. To an extent, though. He didn't think they needed to know every detail.

He thought about Sunshine's offer for therapy. Would she keep their sessions between them, or would she spill everything to the Alphas? Maybe she was required to, because of what he was. Was Fox entitled to any mental privacy here?

He didn't mean to, but he sighed from discontentment at his thoughts. Ahren glanced at him. Fox wanted the Alpha to not mention his sigh, to not try and strike up more conversation on it.

To his great relief, Ahren didn't. He kept silent, and they kept walking. Fox decided that he didn't mind working with Ahren.

They made their way into town. Tension filled Fox's shoulders, and he kept his gaze down at the sidewalks they traversed as Ahren took him to a clothing store.

They entered a decent sized store. Fox looked up just long enough to gauge his surroundings, and then returned his eyes to his feet. Ahren took the liberty of leading him over to the men's clothing section. Fox felt a little better being tucked in between the rows of clothing racks.

"You can pick out a shirt and a pair of pants," Ahren told him. Fox looked around at the clothes beside them.

"Any?" he asked. Ahren nodded. Fox fidgeted for a moment, but then he pulled apart some hangers to look at the shirts, and began to make his way down the row. Ahren trailed him at a comfortable pace, not crowding in on him nor giving him too much space to bolt.

Fox didn't want to take up too much of Ahren's time, and he wasn't picky, so he selected a plain black shirt, and within the next five minutes he found a loose pair of army green cargo pants. He turned to the Alpha when he had his outfit, and the Alpha tilted his head at him to follow. They made their way to the checkout counter.

Fox kept his gaze down again as the Alpha paid for his clothes. Once the receipt was printed and Ahren handed him the bag, Fox's heart grew elated with joy. An entirely new outfit, just for him. He couldn't help the grin that spread over his face as he took the bag from Ahren, and he hugged the clothes to his chest.

"Thank you, Alpha," Fox said again. Ahren smiled at him again.

"Keep doing good and you'll get more rewards like this," he told him. Fox nodded. As they walked out of the store, Ahren pulled his phone out of his back pocket. He read something on the screen.

"Seems like Rishima is ready to have you under her wing. I'll take you to her, she's in town too," Ahren said.

"Okay," Fox replied. He followed Ahren down a few streets. Fox studied the town a little more as they went, and he realized there weren't so many cars and more people walking on foot. He made sure not to make eye contact with anyone, pretending not to see them.

The stores they had ranged from big to small, and were comfortably spaced out from each other, but not so much that it took forever to get from one place to another. Fox spotted a couple different cafes, a greenhouse nursery for plants, a post office, a bakery, a library, and so on. He got the distinction that this town had just about everything.

"I have a question," Fox said as they passed a game store.

"Yes?" Ahren replied.

"I've heard that your pack is very self-sustainable, but it looks like down here you have the same setup as any other town that relies on shipments. And the road my driver took into your territory was fairly busy. Do you have dealings with humans or other packs outside of the territory?" Fox asked.

"We have one busy road that cuts through our territory, where other species travel through frequently. It's more along the edge, however, on the other end of town not too far from here. We do get shipments from outside warehouses for things we can't make ourselves, like certain clothing, hardware, furniture, parts for repairs on cars and appliances, etcetera. For the self-sustainable part, we provide 80 per-cent of our own food and water, and we provide classes for survivalist lifestyles in case we ever do need to shut our borders from the outside world," Ahren explained.

"I see," Fox replied. Lily of the Valley Pack truly wanted the most for their members. Most packs that Fox had gotten captured by didn't have nearly as many amenities as this. But then again, they were a lot smaller than this pack.

Ahren took Fox to the town hall building. He took him up the set of stairs at the end of the hall, and down another hall to a door with a label that read "Board of Education."

Ahren opened the door. Inside was a spacious room, with one long table surrounded by meeting chairs, and a counter with a coffee station and snacks. There were filing cabinets along the walls, as well as bookshelves filled with various textbooks and folders.

An Alpha, Rishima, sat at the table with two Omegas, one male and one female, and a female Beta. Fox stiffened as their mixed scents invaded his nose.

"Rishima," Ahren said in lieu of a greeting. Rishima looked up from her pile of papers on the table, and the other three turned to look at who had entered. Fox avoided making eye contact with any of them.

"Oh, Ahren, that was faster than I thought," Rishima said.

"We were already in town," Ahren explained. He turned to Fox and gestured for him to sit at the table. "You're with her now. I appreciate your cooperation today."

"Of course, sir," Fox whispered. Ahren headed out of the room, closing the door behind him and leaving Fox alone with a new group of strangers.

7, Anodyne

Rishima was probably the least buff of the four Alphas, although still maintaining strong visible muscles. Her skin was a shade darker than Leyra's, and her hair was long and dark and braided down her back. She had thick dark eyebrows and full light brown lips, and a hooked nose. What seemed like homemade jewelry adorned her neck and wrists, a series of metal and wood beads.

Fox fidgeted in his spot, unsure of where to sit. Rishima didn't smile at him, but she held out a hand towards the table in invitation.

"Come sit, Fox," she said. She sat at the head of the table, with the Beta at her left and the Omegas at her right. Fox surveyed the available spots, and decided to pull out a chair that was two seats away from the Beta. He figured sitting away from the Omegas would help everyone get a decent impression of him. He folded his clothes up in his lap and used a slight grip on them as an anchor for his newly-returned anxiety.

"Sorry I couldn't take you this morning, getting everyone ready for the day took forever," Rishima said.

"That's alright, ma'am," Fox replied quietly.

"I see Ahren already got you the clothes Leyra promised, so we don't have to worry about that. I'm supposed to give you a tour, too, but I don't think you want to be carted around the town, so here's this map," Rishima continued, and she pulled out a long folded piece of paper from amidst her pile and slid it across the table towards Fox. Fox reached over and picked it up.

"You can study it so that you have a decent idea of where everything is for when you have tasks there," she said.

Fox was surprised he'd been given a map of their territory. He unfolded the paper and looked the map over. It had a satellite view of the town, with each building clearly labeled. There were highlighted lines of different colors spanning between the buildings and through the surrounding areas. A key on the bottom corner of the map told him which colors meant roads, sidewalks, dirt trails, and streams. It wasn't a map of their entire territory, because Fox didn't see the campsite, bonding sector, training sector, or the farm sector he had heard about that morning. It only showed the housing sector, the

Alpha's houses, the town, and the edge of the territory where the busy road cut through.

Fox stared at the line for the highway, the road he'd been on before he got captured. It only passed through a small section of their territory, wrapping around the edge of the town, and the part that was specifically within the border was only two miles long. The jagged lines that highlighted the pack's border ran alongside that road, only half a mile apart from each other.

Disappointment, frustration, and self hatred brewed inside Fox's chest. If he had been on foot, he could have easily skirted around the edge of the territory and kept the road within sight, allowing him to continue on his planned route of travel without trespassing at all. And if he had just stayed inside the old man's car instead of panicking and bolting, he probably wouldn't have been spotted or scented out right away, and he could've passed through undetected.

He gritted his teeth and prevented himself from releasing a heavy sigh. He folded up the map and tucked it in his lap with his clothes. He was not happy with himself at all.

Rishima, not privy to his inner turmoil, proceeded to give him a rundown of what she expected out of him, and what his tasks with her would include.

Rishima helped oversee the schooling for the pups, who were taught by the three others in the room, as well as by some of the adult pack members. They had two schools, one for the younger kids and one for the older kids. Because of Fox's status as a lone wolf, he wasn't allowed anywhere near the pups, and therefore wouldn't have to worry about helping out at the schools. They also had a youth center, which was basically a recreational center for anyone under 18, and Fox wasn't allowed to work there either. Fox was glad for that; kids made him uncomfortable.

Concerning the town, Fox was assigned the most menial tasks. Cleaning up litter, street sweeping, shoveling snow when it would come, power washing buildings, tending to the landscaping, scrubbing off graffiti, and unclogging sewer drains to prevent flooding during bad storms. Occasionally, if one of Rishima's assistant Betas called out sick, he would take their place for the day and help her wherever she needed it, excluding the schools and youth center.

Fox listened in silence, nodding every once in while to show the Alpha that he was listening. When it became apparent that Fox wasn't much of a talker, she moved on to other topics that didn't necessarily concern him.

Fox could feel eyes on him as Rishima continued talking with the others. He glanced up and met gazes with the male Omega. Dark blue eyes studied him, curious. Fox didn't want to anger anyone by interacting with the Omegas; he assumed he wasn't allowed anywhere near them without an Alpha present, same as with the pups. He shifted in his seat and kept his gaze on the map, pretending to be busy studying it.

He listened as Rishima talked about the upcoming school year, only a couple weeks away. She asked the teachers if they had a better time with longer classes with longer breaks or shorter classes with shorter breaks, and then they moved on to whether or not they should stick with larger exams or just small quizzes, and so on. Fox wondered why he was here.

"As for the survivalist classes... does anyone have any suggestions as to how to get the kids to pay attention and take them seriously? So many of them complain that it's not important," Rishima queried.

"I've suggested a week in the wilderness outside the pack borders, but the parents weren't very happy about that," the Beta said.

"Yes, that's a little too dangerous," Rishima replied.

"Perhaps utilize a rewards system? If the kids have incentive to do well, they'll likely pay attention more," the female Omega said.

"We've tried that before, but a lot of them weren't happy with the prizes," the male Omega joined in. Fox glanced up and was relieved to see that he was no longer staring at him.

Fox frowned at the word 'prizes'. The only reward of survival was just that: survival. It made him wonder how spoiled or ill-prepared the pups were, and how well they would truly fare in a genuine survival scenario.

"If... if I may," Fox interjected cautiously. Everyone turned their heads to look at him. The attention made him draw his shoulders up and avoid direct eye contact. He trained his gaze on the wood of the table. "I- I think, perhaps, if you put them in a real-life scenario of needing to survive against a threat, they will be more engaged. I'm not trying to be monstrous about it, but fear is a very good teacher."

"Fear? You're suggesting we terrify them into paying attention?" Rishima responded.

"Not necessarily terrify," Fox replied quickly, feeling his face heat up at the tone and unwavering gaze of the Alpha. "But if they know what it feels like to go hungry, or be cold at night, or know that there's someone out there with bad intentions and they only have their claws and teeth for weapons, they'll understand the importance of these survivalist classes. I'm under the impression they don't think they're necessary. They don't know what it's truly like, fending for yourself."

"He may have a point," the Beta said. Fox turned his gaze to her, surprised. "Like how birds teach their babies to fly by tossing them out of the nest, maybe we should try putting the kids in mild peril.

We don't have to traumatize them, just scare them a little to open their eyes to reality."

Fox was really surprised now. He didn't expect them to listen or take to his idea so readily. Rishima stared at him as she thought it over, eyes narrowed in skepticism. The Omegas exchanged uncertain looks. After a long moment, Rishima leaned against the table, elbows propped on the edge and hands clasped together.

"How do you think this would fare as a team building exercise?" she asked. Fox hadn't been expecting a question like that.

He shrugged a little. "Sometimes lone wolves team up to share resources or fend off a greater threat. I think, since they're pack wolves, they would band together quickly and focus on each other's survival as well as their own. But I don't know..."

Rishima nodded, still thoughtful. "I suppose we could give that a shot."

Fox's eyebrows raised, his mind reeling for a brief moment. He couldn't believe an Alpha had not only heard his idea, but was willing to use it.

"Do you have any other tips?" the Beta asked. Fox thought for a moment, then shook his head. He didn't want to come off as arrogant by spouting more suggestions on their teaching methods.

"Well, I suppose that settles our meeting. Unless anyone else has issues they want to discuss?" Rishima said. Everyone shook their heads.

Rishima began to gather her papers, and the other three stood from their seats and began to leave. Fox stayed where he was until Rishima stacked her papers neatly and rose from her chair. She leveled her gaze with his.

"Well, we can cut the day short since you don't really need a tour or to get your clothes. You can head back to Leyra's or make yourself familiar with the territory. Do be advised, though, that if you get anywhere near the border, the pups, or the Omegas, you will be punished accordingly," she said.

Fox nodded. "Yes ma'am, I understand. Before you go, can I ask a question?"

Rishima tilted her head at him, considering his words. "Yes?"

"Do lone wolves get any days off? Or do we work every day no matter what?" he asked.

"You get one day off a week to rest and have time to recuperate from your labor. You'll get two days a week if you maintain good behavior. If you get sick, of course, you can take the day off but you must stay in your bunker. Or in your case, Leyra's spare room," Rishima replied. Fox exhaled quietly in relief, nodding.

"Thank you," he said, and she nodded once.

"After you," she said, holding an arm towards the door. By then, everyone had already left and it was just the two of them. Fox understood her caution at having him behind her. He turned and headed out of the room.

He remembered the way out of the town hall building. When he stepped outside onto the sidewalk, he looked at Rishima, unsure if he was actually allowed to wander by himself. He considered the fact that it might be a test.

"Am I really allowed to walk by myself, Alpha?" Fox asked as Rishima headed over to one of the cars parked in the small lot. She turned to meet his eyes.

"You've done well with everyone so far, so yes. You behave very differently than the other lone wolves. I think you can have this privilege," she told him.

Fox momentarily frowned, but he didn't argue with her on anything she said, even though he had questions. "Thank you, ma'am," he replied. She nodded again, curt and precise, and then opened the door to her navy suv and drove away.

Fox was left alone. Without an Alpha, without an Alpha's mate, and without a Beta. He'd had short periods of alone time before, but only when traveling between where he was ordered to go. Now, though, he had no destination.

Fox was accustomed to this. He thought over his options. He could travel around town to better gauge its layout, he could head to Leyra's house and take a nap before dinner, or he could simply wander aimlessly and see what else the pack's territory contained.

As much as he had walked today, he wasn't tired. He could try for a nap, but he'd most likely end up simply lying in bed, sleep evading him, and he'd get up for dinner feeling like he'd wasted precious time again.

He decided to make use of his loosened leash and explore. Part of him remained aware that this might be a test, Rishima's way of seeing what Fox would do without direction or surveillance. This was another chance for Fox to prove that he could be trusted.

Fox took in his surroundings. He didn't want to spend more time in town than he needed to, and the map was enough, so he turned toward a road he hadn't yet traveled. It forked off from the road that led up to the housing sector.

Fox strolled along. He took his time, appreciating the fact that he didn't have any tasks to do or Alphas to be wary around. He gazed up through the tall oak trees that lined the road, and found that the wind had carried some grey clouds over. It only seemed like enough to sprinkle, though, not fully rain, so Fox didn't worry. He kept his jacket on, though.

The road wound lazily through the forest that inhabited the territory. Fox listened to bird calls and scrabbling squirrels. He spotted a few deer hidden amongst the trees. His footfalls were light enough that they didn't hear him, and continued to graze without worry.

Fox noticed that no one drove down this road, in either direction, and no one was walking along it like he was. It was a narrow dirt road, not a two lane asphalt one, so Fox assumed it was merely a larger pathway to some other sector he had yet to see.

As he came around a bend, he found a signpost and two brick pillars that supported an iron gate, as well as an iron fence that mingled with the trees and shrubs. The signpost read "Cemetery." The dirt road turned into it, and a smaller foot traffic path branched off ahead of him.

Fox paused and took a peek through the gate. It wasn't locked, just closed. He wanted to respect the area where they laid their dead to rest, though, so he didn't enter.

Fox didn't think this pack had suffered through many losses. Surely not enough to truly understand how it changed a person, and not enough to hold any sympathy for the lone wolves who'd experienced grief. As he observed the cemetary and its size, he was partially proven right. He peered through the bars at the closest tombstones. By the dates etched into the stones and the type of names he saw, it seemed like most of their dead had died of old age.

Fox couldn't help himself; he opened the gate and entered. The cemetery held no living occupants aside from him, so he had free reign to peruse every tombstone there. He read the dates of each one he could find, and most of them were elderly werewolves. Only a few belonged to younger werewolves, a couple dying from sickness and one dying by suicide.

Fox stopped at that one. He read the name. "Kat Gallegos, Beloved and Deeply Missed Daughter." Underneath that, a line read "Your suffering went unnoticed for too long. We will never forgive our-selves." He read the dates below that, and found that Kat had only been 17 when she committed.

Seventeen. Fox's heart gave a sudden painful lurch, and he turned away. He walked out of the cemetery before the reminder of death grew too much for him.

He closed the gate behind him and took a deep breath. Fox hated fighting, but he hated death more. He hated the absence of a life, the emptiness a person could leave behind and never fill again.

He didn't want to stay here, so he continued his stroll. He went down the smaller walking trail that broke off from the narrow dirt road, tall grass brushing his calves and soft soil accepting his weight. This trail took him a good amount of time to travel. The foliage grew thicker here, and he could barely see the sky above him through the canopy.

After about half an hour of strolling, Fox found himself walking into a very tiny clearing paved by large flat stones, and he spotted a glass door, completely covered in vines. He looked around and discovered that a large building was hidden in the plant life, the walls and roof made of glass, like a conservatory or a greenhouse. There was no signpost stating what this building was.

Fox tilted his head and stepped up to the building. He cupped his hands around his eyes and peered through the glass to get a look inside. He could barely see anything through all the moss and vine leaves. The glass itself was also very dirty.

He caught the scent of something reptilian. He wondered if this was just a nature sanctuary that had once been frequented a lot, but wasn't anymore. This building appeared nearly abandoned, unkempt and forgotten.

Curiosity willed him to look inside. He tried the handle of the door and found it locked. Fox made a sound of disappointment. He didn't have his lock picking tools with him, but he could always just break the door handle. He didn't think anyone would notice a broken door all the way out here, with this building as hidden as it was.

He debated risking it. None of the Alphas had mentioned this building, so he didn't think they utilized it. He sniffed around the area and studied the earth. He could see old tracks in the dirt, and the faintest, faintest smell of werewolves. But neither were fresh. Maybe a maintenance person came out here just to make sure the building wasn't a hazard or housing any trespassers. It was probably only kept locked to keep mischievous teenagers out.

Fox decided he was allowed one rebellious act. He gripped the door handle tight and wrenched it. The metal inside the door broke, and the handle fell apart. He tugged the handle out and dug his fingers in the hole, taking out the rest of the mechanism. With no jamb in place, the door creaked inward. Fox stashed the broken parts in the foliage just next to the doorframe.

He cautiously pushed the door open. Its rusted hinges squeaked. Fox poked his head in and looked around. The building was surprisingly humid, warm moist air wafting over his face. There were tall trees that reached all the way to the ceiling, but they weren't oak or sycamore or pine like the usual trees he'd seen. Their bark was different, and long thick vines hung down from their branches. Wide-leaved ferns covered the floor, and flowers he'd never seen before grew in haphazard fashion throughout the building.

So it was a conservatory after all. One for tropical plants, it seemed, judging by the humidity and exotic nature. Fox assumed it had once been for casual educational purposes, like going to the zoo or aquarium. He wondered why it had been neglected.

Fox stepped inside. He inhaled deeply, gathering as many scents as he could. He smelled reptiles again, stronger this time, as well as the musk from freshwater and the aroma of all the different flowers. Fox wondered if this conservatory housed any snakes, or any other wildlife.

He made sure to be careful and alert as he stepped inside. He didn't want the environment to become disrupted by the difference in air, so he eased the door closed behind him, or as closed as it could get in its current state. There were small stone pathways that wound around throughout the conservatory, partially covered by overgrown undergrowth. He followed them as he gazed at all the new plantlife around him.

As he walked, he would come across small pedestals that provided information on the plantlife. He stopped and read them, interested. As he came across more and more of those pedestals, he wished the pack hadn't cast aside this place. It was genuinely comforting to him, someplace new and fresh and full of life.

Fox heard something rustle the leaves beside him. He froze, listening. He was deep inside the conservatory at this point, and he hadn't come across any animals. But maybe they were hiding among the plants.

Fox peered through the leaves. He couldn't make out what was hidden beneath them, but he knew something was moving. He stepped back, but as he did, he heard rustling just ahead of him as well. He darted his gaze to where some of the wide leaves were swaying, and he saw a series of patterned scales. Mostly black, or dark green, with dull yellow rings. Fox watched as it slithered between the leaves. Out of the corner of his eyes, he saw more movement. He looked up to his right and saw the body of a giant snake, slithering over a branch of one of the trees, high above the ferns and flowers that grew below.

Fox tried to follow the trail of the snake, searching for its head. The body wound around a trunk and another branch, and draped across to another tree behind him. As Fox turned in a slow circle, head tilted back to see the trees above him, he saw that the snake was incredibly well camouflaged, blending in with the shade of the leaves and the color of the foliage. If it hadn't begun moving, Fox wouldn't have seen it at all.

The body grew thicker, wider, causing his eyebrows to rise in astonishment at its size, and then— the snake blended with the torso of a man.

Fox gasped at the sight of a man resting on a branch high above him. His arms were folded on top of the tree limb, propping his chest up. He wore no shirt, and Fox could see the same dark green scales dotting his pecs and shoulders. The man had light brown skin, and long dark yellow hair that reached his waist. A pair of intense golden eyes were staring at him.

For a moment, neither spoke. Fox swallowed down his shock. "Hello," he greeted, uncertain.

A long forked tongue darted out from the man's mouth, flicking in the air before disappearing. "Hello," the man replied.

Fox was very aware of the sound of slithering all around him. He gathered his stunned thoughts and mentally pulled up the information he knew. The man's waist didn't end in legs, but instead the body of a large snake. The conservatory housed tropical plants, reminiscent of a rainforest. Fox knew other mythical creatures aside from werewolves existed. During his homeschooling, he had learned that nagas existed, but were extremely rare; endangered. They typically thrived in harsher environments, such as deserts and rainforests. Venomous types lived in the deserts, and constrictor types lived in the rainforests.

Fox didn't have to worry about being struck by a pair of fangs, but he did have to worry about being crushed to death. Fox studied the naga's face. Fox had been on the receiving end of more than a few predatory gazes, and this man wasn't giving him one. He seemed only curious, his eyes watchful and body relaxed.

"Who are you?" the naga asked.

"My name is Fox. I'm... new here," Fox answered.

The naga hummed thoughtfully. "It is rare that I get willing visitors." He adjusted himself, the snake body slithering faster. Fox's heart leapt up into his throat as a strong tail quickly wrapped around his thighs and waist, lifting him off his feet. He tried not to panic as the naga lifted him high up into the trees so that they were closer, face to face.

Fox marveled at the strength this naga had. He had lifted him like he weighed no lighter than a mouse, and he had no doubt that he could kill him just as effortlessly. Fox forced himself not to show his fear, though. He had a feeling that acting like prey would trigger the naga's predatory instincts.

To distract himself, he asked him a question. "Do you have a name?"

The naga flicked his forked tongue out between their faces. "Anodyne," he stated.

"Anodyne..." Fox repeated in a whisper. He found himself caught in the snake's gaze. His golden eyes truly were intense, especially this close, and they seemed to almost glow. His pupils were partial slits, partial circles.

Fox's hands came to rest on the coils that held him. He felt Anodyne's tail slowly add another coil, slithering up closer to his stomach and chest. The scales slid smoothly under his palms, a gentle rasp. Anodyne could've easily made his grip tight, suffocating, but Fox mused that his grip felt gentle, only tight enough to keep him from slipping out and falling. Fox studied the scales on his chest, mesmerized by their sheen. He was even more enraptured by the way his body morphed from man to snake, skin melding with scales. He watched the way the patterns shifted as Anodyne adjusted himself again, tucking another coil under Fox's legs and moving them up, so Fox was basically sitting in his tail.

Fox brushed his hand down Anodyne's tail. The end of it had tucked itself against his stomach, but at the attention, it moved up and slithered slowly around his forearm, brushing up against his palm. Fox splayed his fingers, and the tail wound around them. It was so interesting to see how flexible a snake truly was.

"How long have you been here?" Fox asked. He realized his fear had melted away in the midst of his wonderment. The thick strong muscles around his body didn't feel life threatening, but more like a comfortable chair with an accompanied weighted blanket.

Anodyne's tongue flicked out again, a couple times, tasting the scent in the air between them. Tasting Fox's scent. "I arrived here in summer. Twenty-three summers have passed since then."

Fox studied Anodyne's physique and facial features. He looked as young as Fox, if not a little bit older. His abdomen and arms held just as much muscle as a Beta. He couldn't remember if nagas lived for far longer than werewolves and humans.

"Were you a child when you came here?" Fox asked him. Anodyne shook his head.

"This is merely my latest home," Anodyne replied.

"Latest?" Fox echoed, curious.

"I was born in a sanctuary, and released into the wild. In the wild, I was captured by different humans. I was kept in a cage, a live trophy in a rich man's house. The rich man died, and I was moved to an underground market. In the underground market, an Alpha werewolf purchased me, and I was brought here. I have been here since," Anodyne told him.

Fox guessed this snake had been around for a long time. "Who purchased you? Do you know their name, or what they look like?" Fox asked. He was very intrigued at the notion that one of the Alphas had purposely bought the naga.

"His name was Oriand. He was... he had some age on him. He had a very young son at the time of my arrival. That son is Evander," Anodyne replied. Fox found his interest further piqued.

"Why did they buy you?" Fox asked next.

"To eat their enemies. To eat the lone wolves who trespassed," he said.

Fox's face blanched, his stomach dropping so quickly he almost grew nauseous. His heart pounded in his chest as adrenaline rushed through his system.

He reminded himself to keep calm, to feign indifference. He swallowed and took a steadying breath. "S-Seems like a lot of trouble to go through just to get rid of your enemies."

Anodyne's tongue flicked out again, gliding between his lips with quick ease. He lifted a hand and propped his chin on his palm, and the tip of his tail played with Fox's fingers. "I have not spent much time with the werewolves, but I am under the impression that Oriand had a dark side. He did not stay Alpha for long."

Fox carefully exhaled. "I see..." This new information on the pack's past made him curious about Evander and the others. He wasn't entirely sure how one became an Alpha, if they were positions that were inherited, or earned by show of strength and leadership. He didn't think it was a good idea to go up and ask Evander about something like that, though. Maybe Ahren would be more likely to answer his questions.

Anodyne calmly tilted his head, studying Fox. "Are you a lone wolf?"

Fox swallowed again. He immediately thought to lie in order to protect himself, but a certain thought crossed his mind just as he parted his lips.

Fox had been heading West for a reason. He'd had a plan in mind, one that he had made peace with ages ago. Fox did not want to die by the hands of others, in the midst of terror or anger. He wanted to die by his own, in the midst of quiet and tranquility. Fox reminded himself that he was at peace with dying, because he did not have anything left to live for. If Anodyne wanted to kill him, he wouldn't be very happy with how he would die, but he wouldn't fight back.

Fox turned his head to the side and gazed at the foliage around him. It was close enough to the environment he'd wanted to die in. No one around, aside from the naga, nature surrounding him on all sides, no one knowing he was there.

Fox took a deep breath, his fear gone again. "I am."

Fox flinched when he felt Anodyne trace one of the bruises on his arm. "You could have lied," the naga stated.

"I could have..." Fox agreed, watching the naga carefully press on the bruises, light and testing. "But I have nothing to live for. If you want to eat me, you can. Just... snap my neck beforehand, so I don't have to suffocate."

Anodyne lifted his gaze from the bruises to Fox's eyes. Golden glow mesmerized him again, holding his gaze in place, unwavering and calming. "Would you say that I also have nothing to live for?"

Fox hadn't been expecting that. He furrowed his brows a little and looked around the conservatory again. The naga was all alone, most likely only fed intermittently, and probably barely entertained or cared for. Anodyne was kind of like him, in a way. Presumably no family or friends, and trapped here for however long he was useful for.

Fox was sure that the naga had more than enough strength to break the glass walls of the conservatory. He could escape if he wanted to, but judging by the difference in environment, maybe Anodyne couldn't survive very well on his own, in this forested mountainous region. He could get by for a little while, but he would need his humidity and warmth. He would not survive a winter outside this building. Without help, he was indeed trapped here.

"I... I suppose so, yes," Fox answered in a whisper.

"Would you eat me?" Anodyne asked. Fox frowned at him. Anodyne held his gaze again. His coils tightened ever so slightly around Fox, but once again, he didn't feel like he was in danger.

"No," Fox stated simply. He had no reason to eat him, to attack him or hurt him. Fox didn't want to, anyway, even if he did have a reason.

Anodyne's tongue flicked out again. Something clicked in his head, and Fox understood what the naga was getting at. "You are the first willing visitor I've had. The Alphas come, but they only come to give me deer or boar, or another werewolf."

Fox brushed his hand over Anodyne's tail, feeling his smooth glistening scales. He couldn't imagine how lonely the naga must feel. Or maybe he could imagine it very well, and he knew how much it hurt to go without friends or family for so long.

"If you're not going to eat me, then... I can come back and visit you more. I can bring stuff for us to do, so you're not bored or left without," Fox suggested. "Do you need anything?"

Anodyne's expression morphed from calm observation to surprised interest. "Do I need anything?" he repeated. One of his hands absently brushed through his long dark yellow hair.

"A brush? Do you have soap?" Fox suggested.

"I have a means to keep clean. But I would love a brush," Anodyne replied. Fox nodded.

"I can bring a brush next time," he said. Anodyne inhaled, his coils tightening around Fox.

"You will return?" he queried. Fox nodded again. How could he not, after discovering him here in this abandoned building, all by himself.

"I will," he said, and he meant it. Anodyne smiled, his golden eyes glowing brighter.

"I should probably head back soon, though. If I don't show up to dinner, they'll get upset and punish me," Fox told him. Anodyne's happy expression fell into disappointment, but it was quickly accepted.

"I see," the naga replied, his hand tracing the bruises again. "I enjoyed talking with you."

"Me too. I've never met a naga before," Fox said.

"Never?" Anodyne echoed. Fox shook his head, and the naga smiled again.

"Thank you for not running away screaming," he said. Fox brushed his palms over the snake's tail again.

"I've been on the receiving end of that before, so I know how it feels. Anyways, can you please set me down?" Fox responded. Anodyne shifted his body and lowered Fox down to the ground, setting him lightly on his feet. When Fox gained his footing, the tail slithered away, freeing him from its grip.

"You are going to come back?" Anodyne checked. Fox's heart ached in sympathy for him. He knew abandonment all too well.

"I will. I promise," Fox told him, his tone sincere. He held Anodyne's gaze for a long moment, and then he lifted his hand in a wave goodbye. Anodyne waved back, and Fox trekked back through the conservatory to the broken door.

8, Just A Conversation

When Fox returned outside, he dug out the broken door handle and gave his best attempt at assembling it back in the door. Obviously the handle wouldn't work properly anymore, but it wouldn't be blatant that someone broke it and stashed it. It would merely be broken, and the Alphas could speculate that Anodyne had broken it from inside.

When Fox finished and he took a moment to look over his handiwork, a brief surge of anxiety and fear seized his lungs. Fox didn't know how often the Alphas came here to keep the naga fed. He hoped that enough time would pass between now and the next feeding that his scent would fade, and they wouldn't detect him as the culprit for breaking and entering.

Fox wondered if the Alphas would be angry with him for discovering the naga, if he was even allowed to know, or if Anodyne was a strict secret. He was afraid to ask. It occurred to him that he would need to wash off the naga's scent in order to keep everyone none the wiser of where he'd been.

He walked at a more brisk pace down the tiny path and down the unoccupied dirt road. He wasted no time in heading back up the road that led to the Alphas' houses. When he reached Leyra's house, he tried the front door and found it locked. Of course.

Fox didn't want to risk knocking and running into either Sunshine or Leyra, and the first alternate course his mind thought of was climbing the side of the house and trying his window.

Fox was more worried about getting caught with Anodyne's scent on him than he was about getting caught sneaking in through his window. He stepped back and studied the house's structure. He mapped out a path, and then began to climb. He was lucky that his window sat right above a small bit of roof that hung over the front patio.

He climbed on top of the patio railing, then reached up and gripped the roof, and used that to haul himself up over the edge. He propped his feet against one of the wood planks that supported the roof and used that as leverage to pull himself up the rest of the way. Safely crouched on top, he crawled up to his window. He scanned the frame and couldn't quite tell if it was locked. He gave it a small tug, then another, and it slid open.

Relief elated Fox. He exhaled the tense breath he'd been holding and crawled inside the spare room. He shut the window immediately, as silently as he could, and tiptoed over to his door.

He cracked it open and quickly scanned the hall. Empty. He listened intently, but couldn't hear anyone inside the house. Maybe Leyra wasn't back yet, or she and her mate were out somewhere else. Fox took his chance and grabbed his bag from his closet, then rushed to the bathroom and locked himself in.

Fox had made sure to grab his new clothes from where he'd dropped them in the conservatory, and had tucked them in the hem of his pants when he climbed the house. He set those off to the side and stripped his current outfit, and hurried to get the shower going.

Amidst the warm water, Fox scrubbed himself as well as he could, twice. When he figured he smelled well enough like soap and not like giant snake, he shut the water off and stepped out. His anxiety diminished somewhat now that he'd had a shower, but he knew he wasn't out of the woods yet.

After drying himself off and putting on a new pair of clothes, he took his brand new set, his snake-scented clothes, and his ripped shirt from his momentary brawl with Seb, and went in search of the laundry room.

Leyra had stated that he was expected to do his own laundry, but he wasn't sure if that meant he had permission to use their laundry room. His safest bet would be to use a laundromat, if the pack had one. Fox dug out his map of the pack's town and scanned the building labels for one. He only saw a small store for professional dry cleaning, which meant he'd have to hand his clothes over to other people, and they would smell the snake on his clothes. They might not even take his clothes, since he was a lone wolf.

Fox sighed. Maybe he could use a quick wash setting on Leyra's washing machine, and by the time his clothes were washed and dried the two werewolves wouldn't be back yet. It was wishful thinking, and it made him all the more stressed, but going in search of a place to wash his clothes would take too long, and it risked running into other werewolves who would question him.

Fox knew he wouldn't be able to go on forever without messing up or irking the Alphas. He hoped something like borrowing Leyra's laundry room wouldn't be enough of a misstep that he'd get in serious trouble for it.

He searched through the closed doors along the upstairs hallway. Right across from the spare room was an office. The door besides that one was a mere storage closet. The door beside that one opened up to a small room with a washing machine and a dryer. Fox exhaled in relief.

He quickly shoved his clothes inside the washing machine and figured out the controls. He found some detergent along the shelf above the two machines and poured the barest amount needed onto his clothes. He turned the quick wash on. The timer told him it would take thirty minutes.

Fox sat down on the floor beside the machine. As it ran its course, Fox laid out his ripped shirt over his lap and dug out a small sewing kit from his bag. The holes Seb's claws and teeth had made weren't too big. Sewing them shut wouldn't be too much of a hassle.

He went to work. Giving himself something to focus on helped keep his stress levels down enough that he didn't become a nervous wreck, but the anxiety simmered along his spine, an uncomfortable companion. He kept an ear out for any signs that the werewolves had returned.

The cycle had managed to get halfway through, and Fox eagerly awaited the last fifteen minutes to finish up, when he heard the back door downstairs open. He froze, his senses instantly on high alert.

He listened intently as he heard someone shuffle around downstairs. The fridge door opened and closed. A moment later, the kitchen sink ran for a few seconds before shutting off. Then, quiet. Fox fidgeted with the shirt in his lap, needle poised to continue its task.

He heard one of the stairs creak as someone walked up them. Fox's shoulders tensed. Sunshine's scent reached his nose first, and a few seconds later, she appeared in the doorway.

"Oh, it's you. I thought Leyra came home early. How did you get in?" Sunshine asked.

Fox stared at her, wide eyed and his heart racing. He couldn't come up with a good believable lie right off the top of his head, so he opted for the next best thing: silence. Sunshine's eyes narrowed, but she kept her smile. After a moment with no answer from Fox, she tucked her skirt close to her legs and sat down, leaning her back against the door frame.

"How about this; if you answer my questions, I won't tell Leyra you snuck in. Deal?" she proposed. Fox felt the faintest sense of deja vu, from when Leyra offered him food in exchange for answers in the prison hole. He figured the two of them made a good pair.

Fox struggled to find his voice, but he managed. "What... kind of questions?" he asked tensely.

"Have you thought about my offer for therapy?" Sunshine asked. Fox drew his eyebrows together and looked down at his lap.

"I... I still don't know yet," he mumbled.

"How about we have a pilot session. A normal conversation to see if we are a good fit for each other, as doctor and patient," she responded.

Fox figured a regular conversation in exchange for not getting into trouble with Leyra was a trade he couldn't pass up. As much as he didn't want to talk about himself, he didn't want to get punished, and that want outweighed the other.

"Okay..." Fox relented. Sunshine smiled in a pleased-with-herself way and adjusted her sitting position, crossing her legs and pressing her toes against the other end of the doorframe.

"What's your favorite color?" she asked. Fox frowned a little, not quite expecting such a light unimportant question.

"It's green," he said, with truth.

"Mine is blue, because it reminds me of calm waters, like ocean waves on a beach or an undisturbed spring," Sunshine replied. "Why do you like green?"

Fox carefully stitched another line through his shirt, "Someone told me once that it's the color of life. And when I look at green, I think of life. Like trees, and moss, and grass. Green means life and freedom."

Sunshine nodded, legitimately listening to his reason. "That's a beautiful way to look at green," she said, and her tone sounded sincere. This caught Fox's attention. "How old are you?" she asked next.

"Twenty five," Fox replied.

"I'm twenty seven. Leyra is twenty eight," Sunshine said. Fox worried that her next question would inquire about the age he'd been when a terrible tragedy struck his life, but she didn't ask anything like that.

"Do you have a favorite animal?" she asked.

"I like owls," Fox told her. "I think it's neat that you can't hear their wing beat and they can swivel their heads so far around. I used to collect their pellets when I was younger. It was a little morbid, but I liked picking apart the fur and bones to try and see if I could guess what the owl ate."

Sunshine listened, still smiling and unperturbed by his remark. "Owls are quite majestic. Personally I'm a turtle fan," she responded. "They can live for so long and there's so many varieties. I used to have a pet turtle when I was a child, but it died. I was so young I can't remember what it died from. I've been too afraid to get another one, like I might unintentionally kill that one too, no matter how hard I try to keep it alive."

Fox found himself genuinely listening, too. It wasn't often that he got asked small personal questions like this, and it was even less often the recipient actually seemed interested in his answers.

"You're older now, though, and you have resources to properly care for one. Why not give it a shot?" Fox suggested. Sunshine shrugged rather elegantly.

"My plants and my job take up enough of my time and energy. Maybe when I retire from therapy I'll get one," she said. "I'm surprised your favorite animal isn't foxes."

Fox shifted his gaze to the floor, his mood taking a downward turn. "I do like foxes, but I like owls more," was all he offered. Sunshine must've caught his shift in expression and tone, because her face grew concerned. Fox waited for her to press for more, but she didn't.

"I see. Do you have a favorite food?" she asked. Fox finished up stitching the holes in the chest area of his shirt and moved on to the ripped sleeve.

Food was a bit of a touchy subject for Fox. There were times he yearned for something specific from his childhood, but no one would be able to replicate the food his mother had made, nor the environment in which he had enjoyed said food. Some food served only as a reminder of his unreachable past, an unattainable period in life where things had still been good, and he hadn't been alone.

Food also served as a strange punishment-reward system, where if he managed to obtain food it meant he'd done something right, and if he went without and fell asleep gritting his teeth against hunger pains, it meant he'd messed up. Food had often been so scarce that Fox had been forced to eat something nasty, and rarely did he get to eat something warm and fresh.

"Not really," Fox admitted. "I consider myself lucky when I get to eat anything at all."

Sunshine's lighthearted demeanor fell more. "I'm sorry. That question was a bit insensitive, wasn't it?"

"It's fine," Fox assured her. Sunshine smoothed her hands over her skirt, not too happy with herself, it seemed. A long moment passed where she pondered something, and Fox continued to fix up his shirt.

"Being a lone wolf is hard, isn't it?" Sunshine asked at length.

Fox heaved a sigh. "Yes. It is."

"How long have you been a loner?" she followed up. Now this was a question Fox had been expecting.

"A long time," Fox told her. He didn't want to tell her anything specific just yet, not until he got to know her better.

"I'm sorry. I'm glad you get to have a decent bed for a while, though," she responded.

"Me too. I'm very grateful I get to have shelter and warmth while I'm here. You have no idea how much I appreciate it," Fox agreed. Sunshine smiled again, but there was less radiance and more sadness to it.

"How are you liking your first couple days here?" she queried.

Fox gave his response some thought. Part of him didn't want to be rude, but he wanted to be honest with her at the same time. "There are some things I don't understand, and there are things I don't like. But I know nothing I say will change anything or make anything better. I'm happy for access to food, shelter, and a shower. Everything else I just have to deal with."

Sunshine mulled his words over. The timer finished for his clothes and Fox set aside his sewing task to move the washed clothes into the dryer. He put it on a setting that would have his clothes dried in another half hour. When he sat back down and picked up his shirt and sewing tools, he could see that Sunshine was still thinking, and still had a somber look on her face. She didn't seem remotely offended that Fox was using their laundry machines.

"I want to say that I feel bad for you loners. But we've had so many come through that were just terrible people, some that I would say deserved the harsh treatment. There are others who are better, though, who I believe have just experienced a bad hand at life, and I wish they could be treated better. You, Fox, are one of the nicest loners I've met. I do wish you could have better. In fact, I hope that in time, you will," Sunshine told him.

Fox didn't know what to say. He agreed with her, on the fact that there were some lone wolves who were downright awful and others who weren't all that bad. He fidgeted with his sewing thread, feeling his face heat up a little at her kindness. She barely knew him, and yet she was willing to wish good things for him. He was beginning to feel bad for sneaking into her house.

"Thank you... I'm... I'm sorry for sneaking in," he murmured. Sunshine smiled again, but there was more lightheartedness to it, and it made Fox feel better.

"Why did you sneak in?" she asked.

Fox still didn't want to admit that he had found Anodyne, still uncertain about how big of a secret he was supposed to be. "I went into the cemetery," Fox told her, "I thought that I would get into trouble if the Alphas smelled that I had been in there, so I snuck in to shower and wash my clothes."

It wasn't a complete lie, and to his relief, Sunshine seemed to accept that excuse with hardly any skepticism. "Ah, I see. They definitely wouldn't have approved of that, since it's a sacred place for our pack. But don't worry, I'll keep my promise. I won't tell anyone, so long as you promise not to go back in there."

Fox nodded. "I promise, ma'am. Thank you."

Sunshine nodded. Whatever sadness had brought her mood down appeared to dissipate as quickly as it had come. "Do you feel a little more comfortable talking with me?" she asked.

Fox thought about it. Sunshine's friendliness had caught him off guard when he first met her, and sometimes continued to do so, but he was feeling more safe with her. Of course, it had only been a couple days, so he couldn't know who exactly Sunshine was. But she seemed kind enough to hear him out, and that was something Fox appreciated.

"If I did agree to therapy, you would have to tell the Alphas about certain things, wouldn't you? Probably everything, actually. Right?" Fox asked her.

"You are entitled to privacy, and even more so with doctor-patient confidentiality. I'm not required to tell the Alphas everything, but I would have to tell them about conversations that hinted you were a danger to yourself or to others," Sunshine told him.

Fox figured that the Alphas would want to know everything he told Sunshine. He wasn't sure if he would actually get any privacy concerning his past if his therapist was a mate to one of the Alphas. He wasn't entirely sure he could trust her to not share the details of his life. Too many times had he been taken advantage of when he tried being vulnerable, or tried sharing his secrets.

Fox drew his eyebrows together. "I try not to remember my past. I don't know if I would be ready to talk about it with anyone, let alone someone I barely know."

"Remember how I said that I care about your story? I also believe that stories deserve to be told. You don't have to tell me everything all at once, but... if anything is on your mind that you need to vent about, or if you just need someone to complain to about a bad day, I would like to be that person for you. I could help you resolve any conflicts you might encounter, or if you have questions about yourself, I can help you understand the answers. I'm here to help, Fox. I'm not here to take your story and run to the nearest broadcast station with it. And I'm not here to use it against you," Sunshine said.

Fox met her eyes and held her gaze. Her brown eyes were so gentle and understanding, so patient and kind. Fox didn't get to meet many people like this. It had always been fleeting, meeting someone who cared. He wanted to give it a try, but he had learned his lesson too many times.

"Is it okay if we don't set anything up officially? Not yet, at least. I just... I just need..." Fox struggled to explain it to her without shutting her down. Sunshine smiled again, though.

"I understand. I need to earn your trust first. We don't have to set up scheduled sessions at my office, but I am here if you ever need to talk," she replied. "I hope I can show you that I'm not here to make your life worse."

Fox blinked and looked away. He didn't expect a phrase like that to hit him so hard, so suddenly. He swallowed down a rush of tumultuous emotions. He didn't realize how many enemies he'd encountered in his life, how many bad people he'd met versus how many good ones. It had been enough that Fox truly believed he was not meant to have a family or a pack. He was meant to be alone.

But he couldn't be alone here. The Alphas wouldn't allow it. He had to maintain good terms with as many people as he could in order to guarantee a smooth life here. If Sunshine was offering to help him do so, he couldn't really brush her off.

"You're too kind to someone like me," Fox whispered.

"You haven't done anything to make me not be kind to you," Sunshine replied. "I can tell you want to be left alone now, though."

Fox watched as she stood and brushed dust off the back of her skirt. "Dinner time is in a couple hours, just to let you know."

"Thanks," Fox replied. Sunshine turned and let him have his space. Fox sat by himself for a while, thinking about her offer again as he finished fixing up his shirt.

9, A Bad Storm

At dinner with the loners, Fox sat in his spot at the end, and Star sat beside him. Seb sat down across from Fox again, and Fox tried his best to ignore him.

Dinner was similar to the food they ate yesterday. A mix of not-so-great greens, leftover bits of meat from rotisserie chicken, and overcooked corn on the cob. Star gave Fox her corn, and Fox gave Star his kale.

"Star," Fox whispered, after they exchanged desired foods. "Do you know what happens to the lone wolves who die here?"

Star frowned and gave him a slightly disapproving look, an expression of "why would you ask that over dinner?" and Fox morphed his visage to one of apology.

"Sorry, I just want to know," he added. What he was truly searching for were any hints that Anodyne wasn't a secret. Star sighed and picked the meat off a chicken bone.

"I heard that we are taken somewhere outside the pack. Hung up in a tree not too far from the border, as a sign to ward off any other lone wolves who might be thinking of trespassing," she said.

"I heard the pack eats us," Seb chimed in. Star glared at him.

"They're not cannibals, you fucking idiot," Star told him. Fox's eyebrows rose in mild surprise at her vulgarity.

"You've never wondered what's in the mystery meatloaf?" Seb retorted.

"It's beef, Seb. We've been over this a hundred times at this point," the lone wolf woman with the shaved head said from beside him.

"That's what they want you to think," Seb countered, pointing his fork at her. There was a collective groan and more than a few eye rolls all down the table.

"It tastes like beef!" Warren said, exasperated. He was seated a few werewolves down from Seb, thankfully. Fox didn't want to watch another fight over an extra handful of food.

"Who's to say we don't taste like beef?" Seb asked.

"Seb," the older gray haired wolf said. "We don't taste like beef."

He said it so matter of factly that the table all grew silent and tense. Fox felt the hairs on the back of his neck stand on end. He'd bitten a number of werewolves before, but only enough to taste the grime of their skin and the tang of their blood. You'd have to rip out a chunk of flesh and really chew it to get a good idea of what the muscle tasted like.

Fox glanced at Star, who glanced back. It was a shared look of acknowledging a threat. The old loner didn't appear to be one, with his age and indifferent demeanor, but his statement alone alerted them that he had probably done something sinister before his time here at Lily of the Valley Pack. Fox now knew not to spend time alone with him.

Seb shut up after that. Fox decided that none of the lone wolves knew what fate awaited them when they died here, which probably meant that no one knew about the naga at all. Given how secluded the conservatory was from the rest of the pack sectors, Fox wondered if anyone besides the Alphas knew about Anodyne.

And considering what he'd just learned about one of the loners, he didn't think he should go telling any of them about him.

~~~
~~~

The next day, Fox finished his shadowing of the Alphas with Leyra. Because he was immediately accompanying her on her duties, he was allowed to eat breakfast with them.

Breakfast consisted of fresh fruit and warm buttered biscuits. Fox ate his fill of four biscuits and whatever fruit the other two women didn't eat, which amounted to a full bowl. The permission had been given by Sunshine, and thus also permitted by Leyra. Fox duly noted that he would need to find a way to thank Sunshine for her continued kindness.

After breakfast, Fox followed Leyra outside. She did his tour first, showing him the remaining sectors he'd yet to see. She showed him the entrance to the hunting grounds, which took up a good chunk of land and extended out past their territory. Because of that, it was off limits to him unless he was with an Alpha. She then took him to an area somewhat close to town and the housing sector, which had a recreation center and a communal cafeteria, where the pack could come and eat meals together, sharing food and ensuring everyone had enough. Fox discovered that this was where the leftovers and scraps came from, which were collected at the end of each mealtime and carted over to their bunkers. In addition to that, there was also a waste sector, which was just their term for the pack's dump. It was fenced off completely on the outside, and had more fences within it that sectioned off specific areas from each other. One section was a junkyard, one was for recyclable waste, and one was for general garbage that would be packed up and hauled away to some other official dump where it would be disposed of properly.

Then, Leyra took him to the farming sector, where another large chunk of land was dedicated to growing their own food. There were orchards for fruit trees, greenhouses for plants that needed more controlled environments, rows of potatoes, lettuce, wheat, corn, and other vegetables, and also a section for berry bushes.

When they reached this sector, Fox was instructed to help Leyra do an inventory check. He followed the Alpha around and took notes on the things she instructed him to write down. His time with Leyra was uneventful, and she was neither harsh with him like Evander had been, nor as friendly like Ahren, but she paid attention to him and made sure he didn't wander off. When he was done with her work, he helped prune some tomato vines and washed the day's pickings with a couple pack members.

Fox was more than grateful to return that evening to a warm shower. Dinner was only leftover chili and cornbread, and yet another fight broke out between Warren and some other lone wolf that Fox hadn't learned the name of. Fox hoped he would be able to keep his spot at the very end of the table, with a Beta posted a few feet behind him.

~~~
~~~

The next day after breakfast, Fox hadn't been given orders on where to go, so he thought today was his day off. He made his way back to Leyra's house, but he didn't want to head back inside right away. He paused out front, gazing up at the sky.

When he woke that morning, there had been a few gray clouds in the distance, but everywhere else had been fairly clear and sunny. Now, though, over the course of the last couple hours, those clouds had darkened and grew larger, and a wind had picked up, hard enough to cause his clothes to billow against his torso and legs. The sky was quickly growing overcast, and Fox knew a rainstorm was on the way.

He worried about Anodyne. Did he fare well in weather like this? Did the thunder and rain beating on the glass walls and ceiling make him anxious or scared? The conservatory seemed sturdy enough, but Fox couldn't help but wonder if its abandoned state made some parts of its structure unstable. He thought about finding a blanket and maybe a lantern for the naga, in case of power outages.

As Fox pondered the worsening weather, he heard someone walking across the dirt street.

"Hey, armadillo," a male voice called. Fox looked down from the sky and spotted Alpha Evander striding towards him. Fox looked around him for evidence of an actual armadillo, wondering how a little creature like that had wandered all the way out here. But when he found no sign of one, and Evander snickered, Fox realized that the Alpha had been calling him armadillo.

Fox frowned. The Alpha beckoned for Fox to follow him. "You're with me today," he said. Disappointment and dread sank low in Fox's gut at those words. His plans to see Anodyne were now out the window. On top of that, his bruises still hadn't faded all the way, and his shoulder and chest were still healing.

"What are we doing?" Fox asked with hesitance, trailing after the Alpha as he continued walking towards the path that led to the training sector.

"Last day of evaluations for the new recruits. Afterwards, we're going to sit down and go over everyone's notes to see who will fit better where, or who didn't make the cut at all," Evander told him.

"Am... am I going to have to fight again?" Fox asked quietly. Evander looked back at him, surveying the state of Fox's healing progress.

"No, you won't have to fight. What I had you do before was only to give you an idea of your rank here in this pack," Evander replied. Relief loosened Fox's tense shoulders. He felt better about following him, and kept up with his long strides, even as the wind blew hard against their sides.

At the training sector, a medium-sized cargo truck was parked by the snack shack. The field laid empty of any recruits, unlike Fox's last visit here. It was just him and Evander, and the driver of the truck who was lounging on one of the picnic benches.

Evander went up to the back of the truck and hauled open the gate. Inside laid different weight lifting equipment.

"Start unloading all this and placing them in specific sections. It doesn't matter where, just as long as everyone has enough room to move around without hurting each other," Evander told him.

Fox was hesitant to carry around so much equipment, but he responded with a "Yes, sir," and approached the truck. He began unloading piece after piece, picking out spots in the open field to place them. Wherever he placed the pieces, Evander began to assemble them.

Fox had to ask at one point. "Is there no gym here?"

"No indoors one. We used to have one, but the enclosed building filled with sweating werewolves caused a den of pheromones, which led to problems of aggressive competitiveness, both physical and sexual. When it caused an Omega's heat to come early and endangering his well-being, we had to shut it down. Now we utilize open outdoor spaces and monitor them. Usually it's here, sometimes it gets moved to the field by the recreation center, sometimes it's borrowed by homeowners to use in their own private spaces," Evander said.

"Oh," Fox replied as he set down another piece of the equipment Evander was putting together. He didn't think about gyms being problems for werewolves, and he grimaced at the image of a bunch of hormonal men and women going at each other, in various ways.

Without much additional chitchat, Fox continued his task. After moving out all the pieces, he then had to move out the weights themselves. They started off light and easy, ranging from dumbbells to rubber plates to sand-filled balls. Fox struggled with some of the heavier ones, but he didn't want to appear weak and useless, so he dug up his inner strength and carried what he could to the field. He did well, lifting with his legs and pausing when he felt his muscles giving out.

The problem came when he went to lift a large tire, suited for intense squatting-and-tossing exercises. It was nearly as big as him, but Fox figured that if he could get it out of the truck and upright, he could roll it out to the field. It was currently on its side in the truck, so Fox knelt down behind it and attempted to push it towards the end of the truck bed.

Doing that proved to be difficult. Fox's shoes slid across the truck floor, the tire not budging. Fox shifted his footing and tried again, managing to shove the tire a few inches. He tried this a few more times until his shoes slid out from underneath him again. He grunted and winced as his knee hit the hard metal flooring.

He groaned and took a moment to let the sharp pain rise and ebb into a dull ache. Yet another bruise for him to expect. Fox sighed and climbed out of the truck. He'd managed to push the tire within reach, so he leaned forward and tugged the tire closer, yanking it towards him repeatedly in quick short succession.

Eventually, he managed to pull it all the way out, sending it down to the grass with a loud thud. Fox made sure to jump away as it fell so that his feet wouldn't get crushed under it. He knelt down and attempted to pull it upright, but he could barely lift it a few inches off the ground. Fox tried again. And again. He adjusted his stance and grip and tried again.

How heavy was this thing? Fox didn't want to be embarrassed, accused of being weak over something he should be able to lift. He had a feeling Evander wouldn't let him live it down, his failure serving as fuel for entertainment.

Fox gritted his teeth and yanked it up, then crouched down and propped his shoulder underneath it. He strained under its weight, holding his breath as he tried pushing it up.

"Fox, stop, stop," Evander said, the Alpha quickly approaching him. "You don't need to carry this, it's nearly five hundred pounds."

The Alpha knelt down and tucked his arms under the tire ring. Thick muscled bicep, deltoid, and pectoral filled Fox's field of view, and then the heavy weight was lifted off him. He sucked in a relieved breath and watched as arm and chest moved to show him an equally muscled back, strong and firm.

Evander lifted that tire up like it only weighed two hundred pounds. He set it upright and kept a hand on it to keep it steady. "Ask for help next time," he told Fox, and he rolled it towards the field.

Fox panted where he sat in the grass, his shoulder throbbing lightly from where the ridges of the tire had dug into his skin. It hadn't even occurred to him to ask for help. Having to do everything on his own came so naturally to him that he rarely sought out assistance with anything.

He couldn't take his eyes off the Alpha, both out of fear and admiration. Those corded veined muscles had the potential to protect undoubtedly, or destroy indefinitely. Fox swallowed and forced his gaze away before he could be caught staring.

After Evander rolled the tire to where he wanted it, he came back to Fox. Fox felt wrung out and tired now after all that; moving all those weights had been a workout for him. "Go ahead and get some water," Evander said.

"Thank you," Fox breathed. He pulled himself up to his feet and trudged over to the snack shack. Inside, he filled a large cup with water and gulped it down. He leaned against a counter and took a moment to regain his energy.

A few minutes passed. The door swung open and Evander came inside. Fox tensed, but the Alpha only poured himself his own cup of water. He leaned against the counter opposite Fox as he drank it.

Fox avoided his gaze, the silence almost uncomfortable. He could feel the Alpha studying him. "You pull anything trying to lift that?" Evander asked after a moment.

Fox shook his head. "Not that I know of."

Evander continued to study him. Another moment passed. "Why didn't you ask for help?"

"I thought you would make fun of me. Turn my weakness into a joke, and get all those recruits to laugh at me, when they showed up," Fox quietly admitted.

"That tire is meant to see who has the potential to gain Alpha strength. The grand majority of werewolves can't fully lift it. Being unable to isn't cause for humiliation," Evander told him.

"Oh..." Fox murmured in response. "Even for loners?"

Evander sighed. "I may make an example or a spectacle out of you loners from time to time, but only when it's necessary. Not for the sake of sick entertainment."

Fox drew his eyebrows together and chanced a look at Evander's face. The Alpha seemed solemn, neither perturbed by the notion of being cruel nor sympathetic.

"I heard a rumor that Lily of the Valley Pack liked to humiliate its prisoners," Fox stated, so softly it was almost a whisper. Evander turned his gaze away to look out the window of the shack.

"It was that way a while ago. But we only use it now as a punishment," he replied. Fox was suddenly reminded of his talk with Anodyne, specifically the part where he mentioned Evander's father having a dark mind, and not staying Alpha because of it.

Fox's lips parted to ask a question, but he decided against it. Instead, he finished the rest of his water. The wind continued to blow unceasingly outside, swaying the trees in an endless moving sea of green. Fox noted that the sky looked darker, gray clouds now navy blue, and no patch of clear skies in sight.

Soon they heard the recruits arriving, and the two of them returned outside. Evander got out his binder of notes, and Fox stood back and watched as Evander instructed them to begin a series of exercises.

The two of them observed the recruits as they demonstrated the extent of their strength. A majority of them bench pressed impressive weight, some had an easier time throwing weights across a notable distance, and others seemed to be stronger in lung capacity than weight lifting.

More than a handful of recruits attempted to lift the five hundred pound tire. Some, like Fox, couldn't get it up past a few inches. Others managed to get it partway upright before their arms gave out, and the tire thudded onto its side once again. Evander noted those werewolves down in his binder.

There was one werewolf who caught everyone's attention. He was fairly tall and muscular, and Fox somewhat remembered him being one of the winners of the wrestling matches a few days ago. He walked up to the tire, took a moment to study it, then squatted down and slid his hands under the rim. He grunted as he hefted it up high enough to reach his shoulders. Fox thought that was as much as he could handle, but then, in a burst of force, the werewolf growled and shoved the tire up, using both his arms and legs. Fox watched with wide eyes as the tire rolled upright, then flopped down onto its other side.

He hadn't lifted it as swiftly and easily as Evander had, but he'd been the only one to manage to flip it over. Fox turned his stunned gaze to Evander. The Alpha had furrowed brows of concentration, mouth set in a focused line. The recruits cheered the werewolf, applauding him on his feat. The werewolf grinned in a smug manner and accepted back pats and bro hugs from his pals.

Evander flipped the pages of his binder and jotted down a couple lines of notes. He didn't seem impressed nor unimpressed, and that made Fox feel uncertain. "Does he have potential to be an Alpha?" he asked quietly.

Evander looked up from his notes and watched the way the werewolf basked in his newfound social status. "In strength, yes. But there's far more to being an Alpha than being able to lift that thing."

Fox accepted that. He thought again about asking his question from before. Evander seemed willing to talk to him and didn't seem suspicious of him taking note of the recruits' strength, so he thought it safe to ask.

"If I may ask... what does it take to become an Alpha? What traits do you need to have? I always thought it was an inherited position," Fox inquired.

"In some packs it is inherited. Here it used to be that way, when this pack first started out. But we noticed issues in ego with Alpha offspring, which effected the way they led the pack. A couple pack members proved themselves more fit to lead and protect than one of the Alpha's offspring, so rules were changed. Being the child of an Alpha can get you a foot in the door, but now you have to prove yourself through a series of tests and trails, and it is a lengthy process. This werewolf has a long way to go to prove he's fit for the role," Evander explained.

Fox murmured an "oh" in response. He figured a pack this big would need to have adequate Alphas to run it, and simple blood status wasn't enough. He thought it smart of them to have more requirements.

He thought about Anodyne again. Nervousness brewed in his chest as he pondered pressing further.

"Were... you...?" Fox tried. Evander beat him to it.

"My father was an Alpha. I had to do a number of things to prove myself," he stated. There was a hint of hostility in his tone, and Fox took a cautionary step away from him. "We're done talking about this."

"Yes sir. Sorry," Fox whispered. He rubbed his forearm to get rid of the anxiety that came from Evander's newly tainted mood.

Fox didn't ask any other questions. He sat down in the grass to put himself at a lower level to Evander, hoping that making himself smaller would ease his irritation.

Over the next hour as they continued to observe the recruits, the wind grew worse. The entire sky became filled with navy blue clouds, swirling fast above them from the high wind gusts. It began to sprinkle, but the drops were fat and heavy as they fell.

Evander looked up at the sky and surveyed its current state. He took a phone out of his back pocket and tapped on the screen a few times. Fox was too low to see what Evander was doing on it, but he hoped he was checking the weather forecast.

After a minute, Evander tucked his phone away and closed his binder. "Recruits! Evaluations are dismissed early today due to the worsening weather. There is currently a tornado watch two counties over from us, and we're expecting severe thunderstorms within the next few hours. I want all of you to spread the word and seek shelter immediately."

Evander's voice boomed loud and clear over the field, and every werewolf paid attention. A chorus of "yes sir"s rang out among the group, and everyone began to quickly disperse. Fox stood as Evander beckoned him.

"Come on," he said. Fox needed no further persuasion. He followed Evander as the Alpha started marching out of the training sector.

"What about the equipment?" Fox asked.

"We'll have to leave it. It's going to start pouring soon, and we don't want to get caught in the storm. If a tornado comes our way it won't make any difference if the equipment is inside the truck or not," Evander replied.

Fox couldn't help but worry how much damage a tornado could cause, no less a tornado hauling around heavy weights, sending them flying in all directions. He grew anxious as the wind suddenly picked up to intense forceful gusts, pressing on them so hard they had to lean against it as they walked. Their hair whipped around their heads, stinging Fox's ears, and the sprinkling grew into rain.

Fox followed Evander to the bunkers, where he instructed the Betas on watch to lock in whoever was already inside and to find shelter themselves. As the Betas obeyed, Evander pulled out his phone again to answer a call.

Evander struggled to speak to the other caller as he and Fox started jogging back to the Alphas' houses. In a matter of just a few minutes, the wind became roaringly strong, the trees swaying in chaotic fashion and smaller limbs beginning to get torn off and flung away from the force. The fat raindrops beat down hard on them, soaking their hair and shoulders. Lightning flashed above them, and thunder followed not a second later.

Fox could feel anxiety fill his chest. He knew that getting caught outside in a storm like this could be life threatening. He'd been through a few bad storms himself, and he'd been lucky to find shelter each time.

He worried about Anodyne again. He'd have to check on him as soon as this storm was over and the watch for tornadoes was no longer a concern.

Lightning flashed again, bright and abrupt, and thunder crashed a split second later, loud enough to make Fox yelp in surprise. Evander swore and hung up his phone call.

"Pick up the pace," he ordered Fox, and he began running. Fox ran after him, out of the swaying trees and across the field holding the Alphas' houses. He looked over at Leyra's house and thought about his bag of belongings, wanting to go get it and hold it close, but he knew that both Leyra and Sunshine likely weren't home, so their doors were locked.

He followed Evander to his house. Lightning bolted across the sky again, thunder following soon after. They reached the front door and Evander quickly unlocked it, and they rushed inside.

Fox panted and shivered in the entryway as Evander shut the door behind them, muting the sounds of the howling wind and pattering rain. Evander toed off his shoes and set them inside a small closet in the entryway. "You can put your shoes in here," he told Fox. His shoes were wet and a little muddy, but Fox felt a possessiveness towards them. He didn't want to be without foot protection if things went south.

When a moment passed with Fox not moving, Evander frowned at him. "You're not getting my floors dirty. Take them off."

Fox wanted to keep them on, but he also wanted to avoid angering the Alpha. He recognized that he was within Evander's innermost territory, too, and as a loner his wants didn't matter. With great reluctance, he slid out of his shoes and placed them inside the closet.

Evander sighed and headed deeper inside the house. Fox took a minute to look around the interior. The entryway was a small hall-way, a tiny foyer, and it opened up into a living room. A wide window spanned the wall to his right, giving him a view of the other houses and the street. A big flatscreen was mounted on the wall, and an entertainment system below it housed a few different video game consoles, and two glass cabinets filled with video game discs. A coffee table and a couch sat facing the tv, only big enough for three people to sit comfortably, or one man to stretch out on alone. On the walls were posters of characters and landscapes that Fox didn't recognize. Along the ceiling were string mood lights, currently not lit.

Evander trotted down a set of spiraling stairs that led up the second floor. He tossed a small towel at Fox, who caught it just before it hit his face.

"You can dry off with that," the Alpha told him. Fox unfolded the towel and scrubbed at his wet hair, then dabbed at the raindrops that still clung to his neck and face. His dampened clothes couldn't be helped, but they weren't fully soaked, so Fox brushed it off. He'd been thoroughly soaked to the bone before, so this slight moisture wasn't much of a bother in comparison.

Once his hair felt dry enough, he searched for a spot to leave the towel. He shyly stepped out through the living room to the open doorway at the other side, just at the end of the stairs, that led to a kitchen.

Here he found Evander spreading out his notes across a dining table. His phone rested screen up with a current weather channel displaying the predicted path of the storm. A rather gothic looking dragon figurine sat in the middle of the table as decoration.

Fox took a moment to look around the interior of this side of the house, too. He spotted more string lights along the ceiling around the dining area, as well as a few gothic wall hangings of more dragons, and some mounted lanterns. A sword was also mounted horizontally along the wall leading into the kitchen area.

The cabinets, countertops, dining table, and chairs were all dark in color, either deep brown or full black. A floor rug with an insignia Fox also didn't recognize laid out across the empty space between the table and the kitchen.

Fox got the faintest inclination that Evander might be a nerd underneath all the rough and tough Alpha exterior. He wouldn't ever say as much, though.

"You can sit down," Evander said, not looking up from his papers. Fox tentatively pulled out one of the four chairs that surrounded the dining table and sat down, folding the towel up in his lap.

Thunder continued to rumble outside. The lightning was constant, it seemed, striking incessantly. Evander finished organizing his papers into two piles and slid one stack over to Fox.

"Read through the notes on these papers. If you think a recruit passed the evaluations, set it to your right, and if you think they failed, set it to your left," he told him.

"Okay..." Fox whispered, but he furrowed his brows as he took a look at the paper on top. It had a first and last name, age, gender, social gender, and whether or not they were born inside the pack or taken in with a refugee family. The notes below this information covered the recruit's fighting ability, agility level, strength level, and endurance level. It also noted smaller details, such as whether the recruit was friendly and helpful to their peers, or if they were rude and selfish.

A thought occurred to Fox as he finished reading. "Sir?"

"Hm?" Evander replied, half listening.

"Why are you letting me read all this information on your pack members?" Fox asked. As a lone wolf, he figured Evander wouldn't want Fox knowing anything about anyone unless it was necessary, and these papers seemed to be handing him some fairly vital information.

Evander looked up and held Fox's gaze. "You have insight that is untainted by pack bias. These people are not packmates to you, they are simply strangers. Your opinion on them gives a refreshed outside view on who they are, which will help me in seeing them in a different perspective. However," Evander straightened up, "I'm entrusting this information on the assumption you will remain docile and not go out of your way to abuse this knowledge. If I get even a whiff that you're using this to harm my pack, I will punish you so thoroughly you'll be stuck in the medical sector for months. Am I making myself clear?"

Fox swallowed and tore his gaze away from Evander's unwavering one. "Yes sir. I understand. I will not abuse this information."

"Good," Evander grunted, and he returned his attention to his stack.

Fox tried to calm his nerves by rereading the top paper on his stack. He assumed he was looking for traits of valor and well rounded skill, so he placed this paper to his right.

But after he did so, clunking sounds from outside caught his attention. The raindrops were heavy and pounding, but as he listened to a different kind of heavy thunking on the roof and windows, he realized that it was hailing now. He stared out the window by the dining table, watching quarter sized hail bounce off the ground and litter the grass.

He shifted his gaze to Evander's phone. He saw only a sea of orange and red passing over a series of counties. "Is the watch a warning now?" he tentatively asked the Alpha. Evander glanced at him, then at his phone. He picked it up and studied the screen.

"Not yet, but it seems like it could become one," he told him. Fox didn't mean to, but he couldn't help it as he let out a stressed sigh.

"If it gets worse we can take shelter in the basement," Evander said. Fox only nodded mutely, grateful to have a second more secure shelter available.

The two of them continued to read over the profiles of the recruits, setting them in accepted or unaccepted piles. The storm outside made it difficult for Fox to fully concentrate, often staring out the window for too long, assessing the danger level of the weather. Evander would clear his throat, pulling Fox's attention back to the task at hand.

Evander's phone often vibrated with incoming messages. Fox tried not to be nosy, but he would glance at the screen to see the names of the other Alphas. They were probably seeing who was safe and who was where, and discussing the possibility of a disaster.

Eventually, Fox couldn't focus anymore. He tucked his legs up to his chest and hugged them, hoping keeping curled up would help his nerves. The rain grew heavier, becoming torrential, and hail kept up with it. The wind outside shook the house. A couple times Fox heard tree branches hitting the walls outside.

About an hour into their reading, the power cut out. It was still daylight outside, but Fox heard the electricity in the house die. Evander turned to look at his kitchen, and Fox saw the oven wasn't displaying its clock.

Evander checked the weather on his phone again. Fox anxiously waited.

"Okay, let's head into the basement," Evander said. Fox trembled momentarily as his fear was confirmed.

Evander stood and gathered his papers, and Fox followed suit. Packets in hand, they headed back into the living room and to a door that sat next to the staircase leading upstairs. Evander turned the flashlight on his phone and guided their way down the basement stairs.

The basement was finished, from what Fox could see. Evander's flashlight illuminated plush carpet and plain walls. On one end of the wide open room were stacks of taped boxes with no labels, and on the other end seemed like a workout setup. The flashlight reflected off a mirror in a bathroom, momentarily giving Fox a silent heart attack as the silhouette of their bodies caught him off guard.

Evander picked a spot farthest away from the workout section, against a wall and next to the stacks of boxes. Fox huddled himself in a corner, setting his papers down beside him and tucking his legs up to his chest again.

"I'll be right back," the Alpha said after dropping his own papers on the floor. Fox watched as he moved through the basement and up the stairs, the light fading as he left.

Fox sat in pitch darkness for a few agonizing minutes. The wind howled outside, the rain and hail droned on with no signs of stopping. The darkness pressed in on Fox, a solitary confinement, and Fox's mind short circuited.

One moment he was in the hole, his first day or night here. The smell of earth and cement filled his nose, and his stomach ached for food and water.

The next moment, Fox was in a shed, hiding from the homeowners and the cold snow, huddling up in a corner, his bag clutched close, his extremities bundled as best they could be, and Fox wondering if he would survive the night.

The next moment, Fox was in a cell. Another pack. Still hungry, still thirsty. A dozen cells morphed together, a dozen different pack scents mingling. So many days and nights spent in captivity.

The next moment, Fox was in a cage, in a dark laboratory, with a dozen other animals and mythical beasts like himself. The barest dimmest light came from the tank a siren was kept in, only bright enough to reveal gray silhouettes and suggestions of shapes. Fox could see the bars of so many cages, so many operating tables, so many scientific instruments of research and torture. The siren swam in endless circles, her scaled body passing over the small light in her tank, creating a slow strobe effect. Jars of dead faeries lined a shelf. Vampire skulls mounted the walls. A dragon skeleton hung from the ceiling. Werewolves younger than him whimpered and whined for their mothers. A griffin laid dismembered on the table in front of him.

A light illuminated the room again, and Fox's heart lurched.

"Hey. Fox, breathe," Evander said. The Alpha set a lantern on the floor beside him and crouched down in front of him. Fox realized his chest was heaving, heavy and tight, his throat dry and terse, his cheeks wet and eyes stinging. He tried to speak, but his voice was gone.

Evander wrapped a hand around the back of Fox's neck and tilted his head down. Fox struggled to gulp down steady inhales, wiping at the wetness on his cheeks. The hand on his neck was warm, a surprisingly grounding sensation, and Fox focused on where he was in the present, and not the past.

It took a few minutes, but Fox managed to get his breathing under control. When his breaths came and went more smoothly, and Fox stopped wiping at his cheeks, Evander leaned back and took his hand away.

"I didn't think you were afraid of the dark. You weren't like this in the hole," Evander mused.

Fox avoided looking at him, embarrassed to be caught in a panic attack while he'd been alone. "I'm not afraid of the dark," he said. In all his time as a loner, he had grown desensitized to it. It didn't make him afraid, just alert. He hadn't reacted to pitch darkness like this in a long time.

"Is it the storm, then? Stressing you out that bad?" Evander queried. Fox guessed that had to be the case. His anxiety and stress over the storm, mixed with the aloneness in the darkness, had caused a lapse in memory.

Fox nodded. Evander just hummed and sat down, leaning his back against the wall a few feet away from Fox. The lantern stayed bright between them, keeping the room safely lit. Fox noticed that Evander had brought a couple pillows and blankets with him.

"Can I take a blanket?" Fox asked in a whisper. Evander nodded. Fox reached forward and picked a fluffy gray blanket, wrapping himself in it and curling up on his side, still tucked in his corner.

The storm raged on. Evander attempted to read his recruit profiles, but stopped after a few papers. He took out his phone, which now had a portable power bank attached to it, and he busied himself on that for a while.

Fox stared at the lantern and hoped that no tornados would come and destroy the territory, and he hoped that Anodyne would remain safe until the storm was over.

10, The Storm's Wake

A foot nudged Fox awake, toes pressing on his side. Fox gasped and shot up, not remembering falling asleep, but remembering the state of the weather before he had.

"Easy, armadillo. The storm's passed and we need to check out the damage," Evander said above him. Fox rubbed at his eyes.

"How- how long has it been? Did the tornado hit?" Fox asked, his voice croaky from sleep. The house seemed untouched from what he could see.

Evander gathered their things, stacking his papers into his binder and bundling up the pillows and his blanket. Fox picked up his blanket and the lantern. "The storm lasted all night, and didn't start dying down until sunrise. The tornado passed around us, thankfully, but the high winds and hail surely left an impact," Evander told him.

Fox exhaled a breath of relief and followed the Alpha up the stairs to the ground floor. Evander tossed the pillows and blanket on the couch in the living room and took the lantern from Fox's hands. Fox dropped his blanket on the couch as well.

He found his shoes in the closet by the front door, slipping them on. Evander took a minute to reset the clocks in his house and check to see if every light was able to turn on. Fox waited by the front door. When Evander finished, he met Fox there and led them outside.

The sky outside was still slightly overcast, with small patches of clear skies in between large grayish white clouds. The ground was damp and littered with partially melted hail, small tree branches, and trash from fallen garbage cans.

Fox could see that Ahren, Leyra, and Sunshine were standing in Ahren's front yard. Evander started heading over to them, and Fox trailed behind. He could see hail damage on the few cars parked in driveways.

The other two Alphas seemed to be in conversation when they approached, but they turned upon hearing their arrival. "Glad to see you survived the night," Leyra said.

Survived the night. Fox closed his eyes at that phrase and tilted his head up towards the sky. How many times had he been uncertain if he would survive the night? Waking up to a new day felt like a miracle to him, sometimes.

Fox took a moment to count all the things he was grateful for. He was grateful the tornado hadn't ripped through the territory, grateful his bag of belongings remained safe and untouched in Leyra's house, grateful that he still had access to shelter and food, grateful he wasn't harmed.

"Same to you," Evander replied. "What's the damage? Do we know yet?"

Fox opened his eyes, but kept his head tilted up, staring at the sky as he listened. "I've already gotten a call that some trees have lost some large branches. One fell over Juniper Road and is blocking car traffic, and another one fell on the Mitchel family's roof."

"There's probably flooding in some areas, too. I need to check on the farm sector and see how bad the crops were affected," Leyra said. "If it's substantial, we'll be eating more meat than fruits and veggies for a while."

"Oh, the wildlife..." Ahren murmured, his tone thoughtful and doubting.

"You think all the game got run off or hurt in the storm?" Evander queried him.

Fox pictured all the frightened animals in the forest entangled within the pack's territory. All those deer, elk, possums, bears, raccoons, all the birds with nests now gone. He could imagine their fear, the panic to get away or find someplace solid and safe to hide. He had been like them before. Fox wrapped his arms around himself and finally tilted his head back down.

"It's likely. Keep a look out for dead animals that we can scavenge," Ahren replied.

Sunshine, who'd been silently listening too, looked over at Fox. She studied him for a moment, a small inviting smile on her face. Fox thought the least he could do was ask how she was.

"Are you guys okay? How is your garden?" he asked, quiet enough to not take over the conversation between the Alphas.

Sunshine's smile widened. "We're alright. My poor flowers got trampled by all the rain and hail, though. Such a shame, too. They were blooming so well."

"Oh... I'm sorry. Can they recover?" he replied.

Sunshine shrugged. "Some of them are delicate and probably won't. Others might. With some care, I'm sure most can be salvaged. How are you? You don't look like you slept well."

Fox glanced at Evander, who also glanced at him, and Fox wondered if the Alpha would tell everyone about his panic attack. But he didn't say anything.

"Storms like that stress me out," Fox admitted sheepishly. Sunshine's visage grew sympathetic, and she reached over and patted his shoulder. He tensed a bit, unsure of how he felt about the gesture.

"I can imagine. Luckily it's passed and everyone is okay," she said. Fox nodded in agreement.

"Do we know if any lone wolves took the chance to escape?" Evander asked, a question that caught Fox's attention.

"All eleven are accounted for. Ethan tried to make a break for it while my group was getting settled for shelter, but he didn't get far," Leyra said. Evander growled under his breath, a displeased noise.

"That makes strike four for him..." he muttered. This had Fox wondering how many strikes each lone wolf got before the pack decided they needed to be killed. Unsettled by this reminder, he took a couple steps back from the group.

"We also need to check on... another thing," Ahren said cautiously.

"I know," Evander replied. Immediately Fox thought of Anodyne. He pretended to be distracted by Rishima and her family, who had just emerged from their house. Two of her youngest kids were squawking about the state of their yard.

"Alright. Let's get the lone wolves to start cleanup where it's needed," Leyra said. "Fox, you can get started here."

"Yes ma'am," Fox responded. "Where do you want me to put all the trash?"

"I'll get a bag for you, and you can just toss it in our bin when you're done," she told him. He nodded and followed her to her house, where he waited out front while she retrieved a large plastic trash bag.

After handing it to him, Fox got started. The Alphas and Sunshine filled Rishima in on their conversation, and then dispersed to help different sections of the pack.

For a moment, Fox was left alone. Partially. Rishima's mate and their four kids stayed outside their house, searching for lost yard toys and picking up their own trash. Fox made sure to keep his distance.

Fox picked his way along the other three Alphas' yards and the fields surrounding their houses. The trash he collected consisted mainly of wrappers, papers, and cardboard. He filled his bag up over the course of an hour, and then when it seemed like the area was clean, he tossed the bag into Leyra's garbage bin.

Fox then took the liberty of gathering up all the torn branches that were scattered around the street and field, piling them up close to Ahren's house. He wasn't sure if they'd want to use the windswept wood for something.

Just before he finished, Rishima's mate took their kids back inside, and a female Beta walked into the area along the road. She checked on Fox's progress, and after seeing he was done, she escorted him into town. Fox found many streets had flooded from the storm, and a few power lines had been damaged by flying debris.

They met with Rishima, who then had Fox go around town and unclog all the sewer drains, allowing the flooded streets to drain. Halfway through his chore of digging out clumps of garbage and leaves, he felt his stomach begin to cramp. He realized he'd missed breakfast.

After his task was done and most of the flooding had gone down, he found Rishima at town hall and asked her if he could find some food for himself. Rishima was happy with his cooperation so far, so she gave him a twenty dollar bill and a written permission slip. She instructed him to head to the bakery and bring a batch back for both of them. The bakery was selling their pastries from yesterday to avoid wasting all that food. Fox was perfectly fine with eating day-old pastries, and happily set off.

There weren't as many werewolves in town as there normally would be, due to stores being closed and the streets being flooded, but there were still some determined people who needed to replenish spoiled groceries or obtain other supplies.

During his cleanup, Fox had kept his head down and focused on the drains, but now, as he walked, he kept glancing at the other pack wolves he passed. Most looked at him with distrust or disgust. Some gave him a wide berth, even crossing the street to avoid him. A few were rude enough to cover their noses with their shirts. A common insult, not because Fox necessarily smelled bad, but because he smelled other, not of the pack.

Fox hurried himself along, not wanting to linger longer than he needed to. He found the bakery, one of the few shops open and running, and stepped inside. He found himself behind a line of five people. Scents of bread and sugar filled his nose, as well as undertones of cinnamon and berries. He went unnoticed for the greater part of two minutes, but as his scent mingled with the other wolves, they turned their heads to look at him, brows furrowed, mouths curled in sneers.

Fox took a deep breath and tucked his hands inside his pockets, keeping his eyes fixed on his shoes. The line gradually shortened, and soon it was his turn. He lifted his gaze to the cashier's, a woman who seemed to be in her thirties.

She raised a brow and looked him up and down. "What are you doing here?" she asked, vaguely accusing.

"Alpha Rishima sent me to get a batch for her," Fox said. He brandished the permission slip and the money, which she took and looked over with skeptical eyes. She looked at him when she was done.

"Hm. Alright then," she replied, unperturbed. She turned and began packing the better-looking pastries from the display case into a box. Fox waited as patiently as he could, swallowing down the saliva that kept building in his mouth. He tried not to appear too eager as she handed him the box and his change.

"Thank you," he said, and wasted no time in leaving. He completely avoided the other pack wolves' gazes as he made his way back to town hall.

He found Rishima in her office, a room in the building that she had all to herself. She was buried in paperwork when he entered, so Fox didn't want to disturb her. Her office had its own little kitchenette, and he set the box down on a counter. He quietly found a stack of paper plates and set two aside. He picked out a pastry for himself and one for Rishima. He set Rishima's plate down in an available space on her desk, then sat down in a spare chair and began to eat.

Rishima still didn't acknowledge him, her brows furrowed in concentration and her pen poised over various papers. But she did reach over and pick up her pastry for a bite, chewing slowly and absent-mindedly. Fox took advantage of her distraction and helped himself to another pastry. She also had a water jug with paper cups in her kitchenette, and Fox quietly helped himself to some water as well. Rishima still didn't notice.

"Alpha?" Fox called gently.

"Hm?" Rishima hummed without looking up.

"Am I free for the rest of the day?" he asked. Fox wanted to have enough time to go see Anodyne today, and be able to sneak back into Leyra's house for a shower afterwards without her being home yet.

"Sure. The other loners are taking care of cleanup everywhere else, so there's not much else you could help with. Just don't get into any trouble," Rishima responded. Fox tried his best not to make his newfound excitement known.

"Thank you," he replied. He wasted no time in exiting the office and making his way out of the building.

Fox took a deep breath as he stepped outside. He was free of chores and errands, now, and it was welcome weight off his shoulders. Just before he set off to go see the naga, he remembered that he had promised to bring a brush next time he visited. A few other things couldn't hurt, too.

Fox had stashed his map of the town in his back pocket yesterday, before the storm hit. He took it out and searched for stores where he could get what he was looking for. Given the fact that most stores were closed and the town wasn't as busy as it normally was, Fox would have an easier time not getting noticed or caught.

Fox tried not to steal when he could help it, mostly just to avoid getting arrested. His years as a lone wolf had made him indifferent towards the immorality of theft, because he knew that the majority had far more than they needed, and he had next to nothing. Sometimes stealing meant whether or not he would go cold or go hungry, and if he had the option to take what he needed, he would.

In this case, he wasn't going to steal for himself. Anodyne had even less than him, and Fox was going to change that.

He mapped out a route to a small general goods store. He could get most things from there. He picked a path that seemed like it would be less traveled, and headed off, veering away from the main road.

The general goods store was closer to the outskirts of town. He traveled through small side streets and alleys between buildings. He kept his map out to see how close he was getting.

He slipped inside the last alley he'd need to pass through. He would just need to walk down to the other end and turn a corner, and the back doors of the general goods store should be right there.

He jogged to cut down on time, tucking his map away in the process. Right as he reached the other end and was about to peek around the corner, a man emerged from his left, coming from an open empty lot behind the stores.

Fox's heart lurched in his chest and he prepped for flight, legs stuttering, but he recognized the man as Warren, one of the lone wolves who'd fought Seb for his food a few days ago. Warren halted and made to bolt when he saw Fox, equally shocked, but then he recognized him, too.

Warren grinned at him with yellowed teeth, and Fox grimaced. "Funny seeing you here. Thought you were too much of a goody-two-shoes to sneak around like this. You trying to steal from the stores too?"

Fox didn't want to answer him, but he did anyway. "I'm just scoping them out," he said.

Warren rolled his eyes. "Sure. Hey, we should team up, keep an eye on each others' backs so we don't get caught."

Fox hated that idea. Not only because he didn't trust Warren, but mainly because he'd tried that tactic before in the past, with different lone wolves, and each time he got screwed over somehow. Either they botched the plan and got Fox caught, or if they were successful, they would take Fox's share and bolt.

"No," Fox stated firmly. "Feel free to go in there yourself, but I'm not joining."

Warren's hopeful and smirking visage fell into a displeased scowl. He scoffed and walked over to the back doors of the general goods store, a pair of metal doors. Warren looked around towards the front of the store to see if the coast was still clear, then pulled out a lock picking tool from his pocket.

"You sure?" Warren checked. Fox took a couple steps back to enunciate his point. Warren exhaled in further displeasure and began picking the lock on the door.

Fox watched him as he worked. After a minute, the lock clicked and Warren opened the door. He stepped inside without another look towards Fox.

Fox sighed and took a moment to think things over. He felt cheated of his chance to sneak in on his own and get what he needed. But maybe running into Warren had been a good thing. He thought about how he was inside a pack and not out in some random town he was passing through. He couldn't steal and make a break for it and haul ass as far as he could to avoid getting tracked and arrested. If he got caught here, there was nowhere to run, and the Alphas would surely punish him severely for his act of theft.

But he still wanted to get things for Anodyne. Fox pulled out his map yet again. There was the thrift store Ahren took him to for his clothes. Maybe there was a bin for unsellable items he could rummage through, or a dumpster he could dig in.

It was his next best bet, and probably his safest option. The pack probably wouldn't get too angry at him for taking things that no one wanted to begin with.

He mapped out his route, and set off. The thrift store was a little deeper in town, but Fox kept to the alleys and the less-traveled sidewalks. He managed to make it to the thrift store without running into anyone else.

The back of the thrift store was where the donation entrance was at. It was currently closed, with a sign stating that it would remain closed that day due to the storm. There were no bins, but there was a dumpster.

Fox sighed. He didn't like dumpster diving, but sometimes it was all he had access to. He looked left and right, and when he confirmed that he was alone, he approached the dumpster.

He hauled open the lid and surveyed the contents inside. It didn't stink as bad as he thought it would, and he found a variety of things. Clothes, bedding, home decor items, a few kitchen utensils. It wasn't much, and it was grimey, but Fox still couldn't help but feel like he'd hit the jackpot.

He pushed the lid all the way open and climbed up the dumpster. Keeping himself anchored to the rim of the dumpster with his legs, he reached inside and began grabbing and shoving aside the contents.

Fox took a couple pairs of socks for himself, as well as a worn down leather coat that had holes in the elbows and the pockets peeling. He dug around some more and found an old lamp with a dolphin figurine attached to the base, a tattered and stained purple throw blanket, a worn down stuffed penguin toy, and, to his delight, a wooden brush. Some of the bristles were missing and the handle was chipped, but it would do the trick.

Fox laid the blanket out on the ground and gathered his haul on top of it, then wrapped the blanket up around everything to create a makeshift bag. He tied the corners together to make sure nothing would fall out, then slung it over his shoulder.

Fox wanted to clean everything before he gave anything to Anodyne, so he decided to head back to Leyra's house and sneak in the same way he had before. With his haul in hand, Fox quickly moved around the outskirts of the town. He stayed out of sight within the trees, knowing that if he was spotted with a blanket full of stuff, he'd immediately be suspected of theft.

He managed to trek around the town easily, and made his way through the trees to the Alphas' houses. He felt less anxious this time around, knowing they were all busy elsewhere and Rishima's mate was most likely distracted with their kids.

Fox climbed Leyra's house the same way he had before, although with a bit more struggle with his haul in hand, but he managed. To his relief, his window was still unlocked. He slipped inside the house and shut the window behind him.

He started a load of laundry to clean the clothes, blanket, and stuffed animal. He took the lamp and brush into his bathroom and went to work scrubbing off any grime in the sink.

Once done with his task, he searched around Leyra's house for spare light bulbs. Luckily, he found a box of them stored in the closet downstairs by the kitchen. He screwed a bulb into the lamp and plugged it in to see if it worked, and he smiled when he saw it light up.

He set the brush and lamp aside, and waited for the laundry to finish. He was a little nervous about spending so much time on his own, without an Alpha telling him what to do or even knowing where he was. But despite that nervousness, he felt like he'd managed to get some semblance of normalcy. Fox usually dictated his own schedule when he was on his own and not held prisoner. It felt good getting a chance to do what he wanted for a little while.

His load was finished within an hour. He gathered everything onto the blanket again, which was now free of stains, and tied the blanket around them. He stashed his socks and jacket in the spare room's closet. Just before he turned to leave, he paused, contemplating his backpack, which remained tucked in its usual spot.

He wasn't sure how late he'd be with Anodyne, if he'd make it back in time to avoid Leyra and Sunshine and wash the snake scent off him before they could smell it. To be on the safe side, he decided to bring an extra outfit with him to change into. It would help hide the scent better if he wasn't wearing the same clothes the snake would rub himself on.

With everything he needed, Fox snuck back out of the house the same way he'd come in.

Fox trotted through the trees. He chose to take a shortcut this time, cutting through the forest but keeping the road that led into town within view, and then veering off not far beside the road that led to the cemetery. He went around the cemetery entirely, following the perimeter of its stone fence until he came across the narrow trail leading to the conservatory.

He did the same thing as he had with the roads, avoiding walking on the trail itself and instead keeping it in sight, but walking a good distance away from it. As he walked, he found himself growing excited at the thought of getting to see Anodyne again. He wanted to make sure he was alright after the storm, and he wanted to see what his reaction might be to the gifts he was bringing.

Fox took off in a jog at one point, wanting to hurry himself along. He stopped short, though, when he heard a man's voice further in the forest.

Fox froze, holding his breath to listen. A tense moment passed and Fox heard a male voice again. "...patched with..."

Fox immediately hunched down and moved through the foliage, searching for a better area to hide. He took extra care in where he stepped, avoiding dried leaves and twigs that would give him away. He stepped only in more moist areas, free of debris, and slinked around the trail towards the conservatory.

He kept his eyes peeled, scanning the trees for signs of the voice's owner. He continued to hear snippets of conversation as he moved. Soon, he saw clothing amidst the foliage. This was where he crouched down as low as he could get. He silently settled his blanket of trinkets onto the ground, careful not to disturb any plants.

"It shouldn't be too much of a hassle," someone said, and Fox recognized the voice as Ahren's.

"Yeah," someone else replied with a tired sigh. "I'm just glad the whole ceiling didn't come down." Fox recognized Evander's voice.

"Mmhm. I'll order some stronger glass and find some time to replace all these panels. For now, I guess this tarp will have to do. I'll check on it regularly to make sure the humidity isn't escaping," Ahren replied.

"Thanks. I still have to catch up on all the stuff with the recruits," Evander said.

"No problem," Ahren responded. A small moment of thoughtful silence passed, and Fox peeked through the sparse bushes he was hidden in to get a look at the Alphas.

"Do you think Fox could come help with that?" Ahren asked. Fox perked up at the mention of his name, both out of fear and curiosity.

"You know the less people who know about Anodyne, the better. And I still don't know how buddy-buddy he is with the other loners just yet," Evander stated.

"I thought you said he was mostly keeping to himself? He doesn't seem like the talkative type, anyway," Ahren queried.

"He does. But I've been told he's made friends with Star, and if she finds out, she could tell someone else, and so on. We'll just have to repair this on our own," Evander told him. Ahren sighed, and Fox could partially see him look up at the plant-covered conservatory.

"Oh well... we'll make it work," he said. Evander turned to head back down the trail, and Ahren followed.

Fox waited tensely as they moved through the forest, watching the glimpses of their clothes and skin, until he could no longer see them. But he waited still, until he could no longer hear them. Even then, he waited just a few minutes longer, just in case, to play it safe.

When he was certain that they were gone and weren't returning, he rose from his hiding spot and picked up the blanket. He made his way through the underbrush to the conservatory door.

He discovered that the handle he'd broken was gone, and the hole left behind had been covered in tarp and duct tape. A bolt of panic shot through his chest. The Alphas knew the handle had been broken. But it hadn't seemed like they were upset about it, nor suspecting him of being the culprit. Luckily, however, this meant Fox had a way to get in without breaking anything again.

He pushed the door open easily. Inside, the conservatory was a little less warm than he'd been expecting. He looked around at the walls and ceiling that he could see from his vantage point. Everything seemed normal at first, but then his gaze snagged on a dark patch of tarp close to the left corner of the building, closest to him. Duct tape kept the edges attached to the surrounding glass and supporting metal beams.

Fox set his extra outfit down by the door, and stepped along the path through the building towards its center. "Anodyne?" he called. Silence answered. He only heard the hum of the humidity machine from somewhere in the building.

He continued to walk along the path, gazing up at the tree canopies above him. He searched the branches for the pattern of Anodyne's scales. "Anodyne?" he called again when he didn't see any.

Fox sniffed the air, but the naga's scent was everywhere. His ears pricked when he heard rustling in the leaves ahead of him. He waited, and soon he saw Anodyne emerge from the plants.

"Fox?" he said. His forked tongue slipped out to taste the air, and he smiled. "You've returned."

"I promised I would," Fox replied. He set the blanket on the ground and untied the corners. Anodyne eagerly slithered closer.

"And you brought..." he paused, taking in the sight of the objects on the blanket as Fox held the edges apart. "A brush! And..."

"A lamp, a stuffed animal, and this blanket," Fox listed for him. He watched the naga slither closer and reach down to pick up the items, looking them over. "I wish I could've brought more, but this was the best I could find for now."

"It's plenty," Anodyne replied, voice light with joy. He turned over the stuffed penguin in his hands and squeezed what remained of its plushness. "Thank you, Fox."

Fox's heart fluttered and warmed at the sight of his smile and the glow in his golden eyes. It felt nice being able to bring some happiness to someone.

"I'll bring these to my den," Anodyne said, gathering everything in his arms. He gave Fox an expectant look as he began slithering back the way he'd come. Fox traipsed after him, following the weaving long tail of his body through wide leaves and tall trees.

Anodyne's den was located towards the back right corner of the conservatory. The plantlife encircled a large pool of fresh water, clean and clear of debris. Fox could see the pebbles down at the bottom, and it seemed to be a good six feet deep.

Beside the pool to his left was an open space of moss and stones. Here was where Anodyne laid out the blanket, brush, and toy. He took the lamp and went to find an outlet along the wall next to his den.

As he searched for a spot to keep his lamp, Fox looked around the space. He spotted a small crate of books nestled between two stones.

He crouched down beside it and read the titles. They appeared to be adventure books, epics ranging from two inches to four inches thick. This was probably what Anodyne kept occupied with to not die of boredom.

How many times had he read those books, though? The pages were yellowed, the covers tattered at the edges, the font old and faded. Fox sighed. He wished he had found more things to enrich the naga.

Anodyne returned. His long snake body continued to slither around the den, part of it dipping into the pool, some of his tail coiling and piling around Fox where he crouched, and the rest circling the space of moss. Anodyne picked up the brush and began tending to his golden hair.

"Were you scared last night?" Fox asked him, sitting down amongst the snake body surrounding him. Anodyne looked up at the glass ceiling.

"A little. Storms are common here, but not usually so violent. I did get scared when I heard the ceiling break. Evander says it was due to hail damage on weak glass. They plan to replace everything, to make the structure more sturdy," he said.

"I'm glad. I was worried you could get hurt," Fox replied.

"I was worried, too. But after the glass broke, I was simply cold. I stayed in the water and waited for the storm to end," Anodyne told him. Fox looked at the pool, imagining the naga's entire form piled within it.

Fox remembered the stress of last night and released a heavy breath to get rid of those nerves. Anodyne's body curled a bit tighter around him, tucking him into his coils.

"Do you only have these books to occupy yourself with?" Fox asked.

"Yes. There is not much for someone like me to do besides read. I cannot leave, and the humidity is not good to keep lots of electronics in," he said.

"Maybe I could bring some puzzles, or board games?" Fox suggested. Anodyne smiled at him as he continued to brush his hair.

"That would be nice," he replied. "My old captor used to play chess and mahjong with me."

"Was he decent to you? Or were you treated badly?" Fox asked, genuinely curious. He figured that being kept as a trophy by a rich man had meant that Anodyne was neglected, or possibly abused. Maybe his own past bled too much into his assumptions.

Anodyne took a moment to reminisce. The brush glided through his long hair slowly, thoughtfully. "At times he was decent. Lonely,

I think, and sometimes only had me for company. But when he had company in the form of humans, he wasn't so decent. I was often taunted and harassed for their amusement."

Fox drew his eyebrows together. "I'm sorry."

Anodyne made a gracefully dismissive gesture. "I am not there anymore. I am here. You are here."

Fox felt his cheeks flush, and he looked down at his lap.

"Your life has not been so nice either, has it?" Anodyne prompted. Fox tucked his hands in his lap and began to pick at some loose threads on his clothes. He shook his head.

The section of Anodyne's body that was piled around Fox shifted tighter and closer. A coil slithered over his crossed legs and hands, breaking away his current fidget and making him look up at Anodyne's face again.

Anodyne was looking at him like he already knew Fox's entire life story. It wasn't often that Fox was met with such thorough understanding from someone. Not even Sunshine seemed to extend this much towards him, but then again, she hadn't suffered in her life. None that Fox could tell.

"I don't like to remember it," he admitted softly.

"You don't have to tell me if you don't wish to," the naga responded. A wave of relief washed through Fox, and he felt his shoulders sag.

"Let it stay in the past," Anodyne added. He shifted his body again to pile his closest coils underneath him, creating a bed that he rested in. He laid back against his own coils and switched the section of hair he was brushing.

"Do you want more books than this?" Fox asked, attention brought back to them. Anodyne shifted his gaze to the crate, pondering them.

"Yes, actually. And... if possible..." he replied, trailing off in uncertain thought.

"If I can manage it, I'll bring it for you," Fox assured him. "What would you like?"

Anodyne met Fox's eyes again. "Music."

Who wouldn't desire music when kept alone for so long? Books and games could only do so much. Music was a good companion when warm bodies were absent.

"I'll do my best to find some," Fox told him. Books he could get from the library. Games he could get from the thrift store. Music, however, might be more difficult to find. But Fox would find it for him.

Anodyne smiled again, and something occurred to Fox. "Why does Evander not bring anything else for you, other than food?"

Anodyne hummed, and then shrugged a little. "Oriand was a strict Alpha. I imagine he was an even stricter father. Even now as he is no longer here in this pack, and no longer an Alpha, Evander still obeys him. Oriand believed that giving me luxury items would develop a bond between me and the werewolves, and the werewolves would let their guard down around me, and I would seize the opportunity to eat them when they weren't expecting it. Oriand saw me as only a predator with a brain, not a sentient being with needs and feelings. Things have gotten better since Oriand left, but the Alphas are still cautious about getting too comfortable with me, and with letting me get too comfortable with them."

Fox took in his words and mulled them over, letting them soak in his mind. He learned a bit more about Lily of the Valley Pack's history, and more of the Alphas. He didn't like that they were scared into believing that Anodyne wasn't on the same level of intelligence and sentience as them, or was too controlled by his instincts to be integrated into their society. Maybe Anodyne did have some lesser control over his desire to feed on live creatures, but werewolves had once been the same way. It was only when their species began indulging more in human niceties that they grew less bloodthirsty and wild and developed their modern equilibrium that Ahren had mentioned. Why did they believe that Anodyne couldn't learn to do the same?

"I'm sorry that you're not treated better than you should be," Fox murmured. He turned his hand up underneath Anodyne's coil in his lap and ran his palm along the scales. Anodyne was no monster. He was just lonely.

"Tell me..." Anodyne prompted, leaning forward and propping his arms atop his snake body that circled him. He stopped brushing his hair but still held the brush loosely in his fingers. His long hair fell over his shoulders and chest, prettier now that it had been tended to. "Why does your kind hate their own kind?"

Fox assumed he meant the divide between pack wolves and lone wolves. "Wolves are meant to live with families, with packs. When wolves spend too much time without their packs, they lose themselves. And over time, it gets much harder to get their true selves back. They're reduced to survival instincts and self preservation. Packs are focused on each other, on the good of the community. Living life only benefiting yourself goes against that nature. Often it gets so bad that we become... monsters."

"You don't seem so monstrous," Anodyne said.

"I try not to be," Fox said, and he meant it.

"Do you think this pack would ever view us as anything other than monsters-to-be?" Anodyne asked. His tone was soft and lightly sorrowful. "Because I feel as though you do not deserve to be beaten up."

Fox ran a hand down his arm, reminded of his bruises. They were almost gone now, but some were still visible. "I don't know. Probably not." He lifted his gaze to the naga's. But Anodyne didn't seem dismayed, just solemnly accepting of facts.

"I'm glad you don't see me as a monster," Anodyne said. "Perhaps we can be each other's refuge in isolation."

Fox managed a small smile. "I would like that."

11, FULL MOON PARTY

Fox managed to make it back to Leyra's in time to take a shower without anyone being home. Afterwards, he sat on the back steps outside and awaited to be let inside the house under proper terms.

Sunshine came home first, and found him in the backyard when she went to check on her plants.

"Hello Fox. How long have you been waiting?" she greeted.

"Probably an hour," Fox replied, uncertain about how long it had actually been.

"Oh. Well I appreciate that you didn't sneak in like last time. I'm in the mood for some apple cider, would you like some?" she asked. Guilt pooled in his gut, because he had snuck in, but he reminded himself that it had been for his own safety, and the guilt withered.

"Sure. Thank you," he said, and rose from his spot as Sunshine returned inside. Fox hadn't had a mug of something truly warm and filling since last winter, when he managed to get his hands on someone's unattended drink in a cafe.

Inside, Fox sat down at the dining table and waited patiently as Sunshine began making three mugs of apple cider. Not long into her task, Leyra came home. Fox felt a little less relaxed with her here, worried that somehow she knew about his plan to steal from the store, even though he hadn't actually stolen anything. But as she toed off her shoes and hung up her thin jacket, she only seemed tired.

"Hello my starling," Sunshine greeted cheerfully as Leyra trudged into the kitchen. Leyra hugged her waist and buried her face in Sunshine's shoulder. Sunshine reached up and cupped her hand over Leyra's head. "Was today not a good day? How is the farm?"

"Most of the crops were destroyed. The greenhouses remained in tact, thankfully, but everything outside and unprotected has been ruined in some way. The harvests for those crops are going to be much smaller this fall," Leyra murmured. Fox drew his eyebrows together, worried about what that could mean for the pack. If they had less food to go around, that would mean less food for the loners.

"Is it still enough for everyone, though?" Sunshine asked, finishing with the apple cider. Leyra let her go as Sunshine handed her a mug, and then brought the other two to the dining table.

"It should be, but barely. We'll have to focus on rationing this winter. No overzealous feasts, save for the holidays," Leyra said as Sunshine set a mug down in front of Fox. He whispered his thanks again and pressed his palms to the mug, feeling its welcome warmth. Leyra and Sunshine sat down in the other two chairs, and Leyra looked at Fox.

"What were you up to after your chores here?" she asked him.

"Alpha Rishima had me unclog the sewer drains in town to reduce the flooding, and after that she let me go, so I explored for a little while," he said as nonchalantly as he could, even as he felt his heart spike at his partial lie.

"Hm. Explore where?" she asked. This was where Fox needed to be careful. He didn't know where Ahren and Evander had been for most of the day, and if he said he was somewhere that they were, and they later said they never saw him, he would be in trouble.

Fox assumed they had helped around the housing sector for damages to homes. "I walked through town a bit more, and then I found my way to an empty park."

"I see," Leyra said, and Fox slowly released a breath. "Did you happen to come across the commotion that happened in town?"

"Commotion?" Fox echoed, confused.

"Warren was caught trying to shoplift. I wonder if you saw it," Leyra said. She rested her elbows on the table and interlaced her fingers under her chin. She watched him closely. Fox was glad he hadn't gone into the general goods store after all, with or without Warren.

"Oh. I... I ran into him, but that was before he did anything," Fox replied. He figured he would need to slip some amount of truth into his story if he was going to be believed.

"You didn't find it suspicious that he was sneaking around without any Betas or Alphas keeping an eye on him?" Leyra asked next, her tone slowly growing accusing. Fox looked down at his mug and anxiously rubbed his fingers against it.

"He- he did tell me what he was going to do, but I didn't want to start a fight with him, so I didn't get in his way," Fox said. It wasn't necessarily the truth, but it was an honest scenario of what Fox would've done if the interaction had gone any differently.

"Hm," Leyra hummed again. "I can understand that reasoning. But next time, tell someone, instead of turning a blind eye and avoiding the trouble entirely."

"Yes ma'am," Fox whispered. It hadn't occurred to him to go tell someone, especially someone inside the store, of what Warren was doing.

Fox felt wary about drinking his cider now, like he was still somehow in trouble, and helping himself would make Leyra upset with him. Sunshine had made it for him, but he didn't feel like it was his.

Sunshine started up conversation with Leyra again, taking the heat off Fox, but Fox only sat there, rigid and silent, as his cider gradually got colder.

~~~

That night for dinner, Fox noticed that Warren was absent. He tensely ate his food and tried not to make eye contact with any of the other loners, worried that somehow they knew that Fox had chosen not to steal with Warren and watch his back. Fox wanted to remain on the pack's good side as much as possible, but he knew that meant making enemies with the loners who took loyalty too seriously.

The next morning, Warren was at the table with everyone. He was the last to arrive and sit down, and Fox wanted to avoid looking at him, but his gaze caught on something that made his blood turn to ice.
~~~

Warren's hands, wrists, and forearms were covered in lacerations, deep enough to require stitches. Shades of irritated red blended with the black stitches, inflamed skin mixed with scabs. Even his fingers had tiny cuts over them, his knuckles split and perpetually exposed anytime Warren needed to flex his fingers. There were no bandages to keep the cuts covered as they healed, and Fox had a feeling it was to send a message to the rest of the lone wolves. Theft was always a punishable crime.

Fox swallowed and chanced a look at Warren's face. It was twisted in a pained grimace, teeth gritted and brows knitted together. He must've felt Fox's gaze, because he looked over and caught it. His pained expression morphed into one of rage. Because Fox hadn't agreed to watch his back, Warren got caught. Fox had just made another enemy.

Fox knew it wasn't his fault that Warren was punished for stealing, but he knew that wasn't how lone wolves' thought processes operated. If you didn't help them and they ate shit because of it, their consequences were your fault.

Fox finished his meal with his eyes on his food and nowhere else.

~~~

The following Friday, Fox was with Ahren. He met him at his house, where the Alpha waited, leaning against the side of a truck parked in his driveway.
~~~

"What are we doing today, sir?" Fox asked as he approached him.

"We're setting up for tonight's bonding party," Ahren replied. He tilted his head towards the passenger side door for Fox to get in. The two of them climbed into the truck. Ahren rolled the windows down after he started the engine, and Fox leaned against the door to feel the fresh air. There was no sign of potential storms today, and Fox hoped it would mean a clear calm night.

Ahren drove them to a section of the town dedicated to storage units, and here Fox helped him pile supplies into the truck that they would need for the particular theme that night. "It's going to be a full moon, which means tonight is cultural rememberance themed," Ahren explained.

Fox grunted as he hefted a large table into the bed of the truck. "Cultural rememberance?" he echoed.

Ahren stacked a box of traditional outdoor lanterns on top of a box of traditional festivities decorations. "We'll feast on the catch Leyra's hunting party will bring in, and we'll have music based on our more good-natured Irish origins."

In his homeschooling, Fox had learned that there were quite a few origins of werewolves, and the most valiant one was the faoladh of Ireland. Rather than being bloodthirsty beasts of the night, the faoladh would leave gifts of food for those who were poor and of good character. They were the werewolves most descendants strove to take after in this day and age.

Fox tried to picture what a party like that would be like. He was certain the lone wolves wouldn't be allowed to attend, but maybe he would be able to watch and listen to the music from a distance.

The two finished packing up the supplies, and Ahren drove them over to the bonding sector. The field laid bare and empty like the first time Ahren showed it to Fox, although there was a wooden stage at the far end and a series of large wooden posts encircling the clearing, spaced evenly apart.

Ahren and Fox got to work. They set up tables on which to place the feast, and set up barrels of wine and juice beside them. Then they began hanging up fairy lights and traditional lanterns between the large wooden posts. In the middle of the clearing, Ahren placed large stones in a circle, and they gathered chopped wood into it to make a bonfire. Smaller torches were placed in other areas, such as beside the wooden stage, the tables, and the entrance of the bonding sector. They decorated the entrance with vines and flowers, creating an archway of plants.

By the time they finished with that part, a small group of two Betas and four Omegas arrived in another truck, this one carrying wooden sculptures of various sizes. Fox glanced at Ahren as the truck pulled in to the spot beside Ahren's. Fox wasn't sure how Ahren would feel about letting Omegas around him.

Ahren didn't seem worried, however. He smiled as the group hopped out of the truck. "Just in time," he said as way of greeting. The two Betas approached with ease, but the Omegas noticed Fox and hung back a bit in caution.

Fox kept his distance as the Alpha and Betas engaged in conversation. He pretended that the Omegas weren't there, instead surveying their handiwork thus far. It seemed meager, but some more decorations would spruce the place up.

"Fox," Ahren called, snapping Fox's attention back. "Want to start unloading everything?"

Fox nodded silently and walked over to the truck. He avoided looking at the Omegas, even as they skirted away from his perceived path and closer to the others. He opened the bed of the truck and started unloading the wooden sculptures. Amidst the sculptures, he also found instrument cases.

As Fox unloaded everything, the Betas and Ahren carried the sculptures to open spaces around the clearing, and they took the instrument cases to the stage, where the Omegas began carefully assembling and organizing the instruments.

There were still a few boxes of decorations, and Fox helped to put them up around the rest of the clearing. By the time everything was in place, it looked like a proper Celtic festival, minus the food and open fire.

"Fantastic job everyone," Ahren said as he looked around the area. He looked proud and excited for the night to come. Fox had mixed feelings as he gazed around the field. Part of him didn't like the idea of so many people converged in one area, and the other part of him felt a sting of jealousy at the fact that he wouldn't get to experience anything like this. His own kin wouldn't allow it.

"Am I relieved, sir?" Fox quietly asked. Ahren turned to him.

"For now, yes. But later tonight when the party starts, I'd like for you to help dish out food and drinks with Star," Ahren said. Surprise had Fox lifting his gaze to the Alpha's.

"Me and Star? We're allowed to be here?" he asked. At Ahren's nod, Fox frowned. "Will the other lone wolves be here?"

Ahren's visage grew less relaxed. His eyebrows and the skin around his eyes tightened a bit. "No. They will be locked in their bunkers for the night," he said. He spoke slightly more slowly, almost as if he didn't like the taste of his words. Fox wasn't sure what to make of that.

"Why us, then?" he asked. Ahren's smile returned.

"The two of you are the most well-behaved of the loners, and the least aggressive," he answered.

Fox couldn't help but feel curious about this. He was glad for the chance to witness the party and bask in the outskirts of its fun, but something nagged at his mind, like this sort of thing wasn't acceptable, no matter how obedient he and Star were.

"How will your pack feel about it?" he asked. Ahren turned his head to look at the Omegas, who were now beginning their rehearsals of the songs they were going to play.

"They won't be happy, I'll admit." Fox could already feel their judgment sinking in his gut. "But you'll be there to serve them, not necessarily partake, so I don't think they'll put up too much of a fuss about it."

Fox hoped that Ahren's faith in his pack's leniency would hold true, because he did not want to deal with being called slurs and given dirty looks all night. Or worse, subjected to their entertainment.

Fox reminded himself that he needed to show gratitude, even despite his worries. He tilted his head down in a small bow. "Thank you for allowing me to attend, Alpha."

Ahren chuckled, and Fox flinched as the Alpha ruffled his hair, not expecting the gesture. "No need for theatrics. Just keep being good."

"Yes sir," Fox replied.

~~~

Fox spent his free time in Leyra's spare room, his anxiety slowly growing worse as each hour ticked by. First he showered to distract himself and clean himself from the day's labor. Then he brushed his teeth, although he hadn't eaten dinner yet. He checked his teeth and scrutinized their not-so-white appearance, even though he'd been fortunate enough for straight rows. Then he picked at his hair, messing it up in the mirror and attempting to style it, only to mess it up again.

When he grew frustrated with his looks, he left the bathroom and tried to take a nap. He managed twenty minutes before he was left tossing and turning in the bed, thoughts slowly beginning to pile on top of each other. Soon the normally comfortable bed felt too hot, the blankets too heavy, the pillows too askew. He swung himself out of bed and began to pace, rubbing at his arms.

How badly could the pack react to him being there? How quickly could things go south? What right or wrong things could he say? What if his option for silence was misinterpreted? Would the Alphas intervene if the pack chose to drag him from his position of serving
~~~

food and drinks, and force him to do things he didn't want to do? What if he was put in an awful spotlight and ordered to leave, to lock himself in Leyra's house, or even one of the prison holes?

Soon Fox couldn't take it. He sought out his backpack, digging out the maps of all the parks he'd been to, and studied them. He let himself remember his trips, all the places he'd been across the country. All the people he'd met, all the close calls he'd had, all the sights he'd seen.

It was rare that reminiscing left a positive impact on Fox. He found himself calming down the more he remembered. He'd gained so many terrible memories, but he'd also gained some good ones. Through all the places he'd gone, and all the people he'd met, he had persevered. Through highs and lows, he'd survived. He had worked himself out of every situation he'd been in, and he could do it again. He was a loner. He knew how to take care of himself.

Fox took some deep breaths. He told himself that no matter how the night went, it was just one night, and it would pass, and the world would move on.

Fox laid down on the carpeted floor, holding his maps on his chest and focusing on breathing, until someone came knocking on his door.

He opened it to find Sunshine there. She wore a lovely green dress with black lace along the collar and sleeve hems. The pattern was plain, but hinted at elegance. She was also wearing makeup, which caught Fox off-guard.

"Hello, Fox. Are you feeling alright? Ready to head out?" she greeted. Fox looked down at his plain casual clothing. Black cargo pants and a navy blue shirt. It wasn't exactly party attire.

Sunshine must've guessed his concern, because she waved him off. "You look fine. You're allowed to wear whatever you like, so long as it's not provocative."

Fox still blushed in embarrassment, though. "If you say so."

Sunshine smiled at him, her radiance soothing his nerves for once. He managed a small smile back, and that was enough for her.

The two left the house and walked down the paths leading to the bonding sector. The setting sun warmed his exposed skin, and a cool breeze kept his breaths calm. Fox expected to see more people on the way there, but it seemed the party had yet to start. As he and Sunshine approached the bonding sector, the only ones there were the musicians, a handful of Betas, the Alphas, and Star.

Star smiled when she laid eyes on him, and gave Fox a small wave. She stood next to Evander, who was speaking to one of the Betas that Fox recognized as one of the few who guarded the bunkers.

Sunshine gave Fox a parting smile of encouragement and left his side. Fox trudged over to Star and Evander. Star raised her eyebrows as he neared, showing her surprise at the situation. "Can you believe this?" she whispered. Fox shook his head and shrugged his shoulders.

Fox looked around the field. Not much had changed since he left, although there were a few adjustments made to the placements of the wooden animal sculptures. Someone had hung up a big sheet near the edge of the clearing, and Fox wasn't sure what it was for.

About ten minutes later, Leyra and her hunting party arrived with their catch. They had managed to kill an elk buck and multiple geese. Fox's mouth filled with saliva at both the sight and the smell of the fresh game. How refreshing that food would be compared to the scraps he'd been eating.

But Fox checked himself. He couldn't risk indulging his instincts right now. He needed to be as docile as possible, both to attract less attention and to convince the Alphas he was civilized enough to be here.

Star groaned quietly beside him. Her feet scuffed the grass in agitation. She wanted that food as much as he did.

"We can't," Fox reminded her in a whisper. Star sighed and scrunched her nose in frustration.

They waited next to Evander as the hunting party laid out the food on the large dining tables. They divided up the elk into parts; legs, inner organs, chest, and head. They sliced open the geese and shed as many feathers from the skin as they could.

The sight of all the gore and blood made unwanted memories attempt to surface in Fox's mind, but he pushed them down and dug up his moral indifference to keep them smothered. This was the way of things, life feeding life. This wasn't for anything else.

Everyone preferred their meat differently, so Fox and Star were instructed to cut up the portions according to what a pack member asked for. They would also keep track of who was drinking juice and who was drinking wine, and how much wine someone was having over the course of the night, just to keep track of who could become a drunken problem.

Evander finished up his conversation with the bunker guard Beta, and turned to the two loners. He met their gazes with a strong glare and pointed a finger at them. "The two of you are not here to party. You're here to serve the pack, and that's it. If I catch either of you helping yourselves to our food, or you try to sneak off and cause trouble somewhere, your ass is getting a beating right here in front of everyone. Do not disrespect anyone, try to start a fight, or try to sexually assault anyone. There will be eyes on you all night, so behave."

A sting of offense shot through Fox's chest at Evander's words, especially the accusation of potentially assaulting someone. Fox didn't think he gave off any rapist vibes, but maybe just being a lone wolf in general made everyone wary of him committing that very atrocity. He furrowed his brows and tilted his head down. He murmured a "yes, Alpha, I understand," while Star remained silent next to him. She only nodded mutely in agreement, her gaze also on the ground.

Evander made a gruff growling noise of dismissal before turning away and finding his place among the other Alphas. Fox released a slow breath. He hoped tonight wouldn't be a bad one.

Dusk slowly faded into night. The full moon shone in all its lunar glory, mingling with the firelight that gradually lit the field. One by one, group by group, pack wolves arrived. The bonfire was kindled and set alight, providing radiant warmth to the clearing. The musicians took up their instruments on the wooden stage and began to play melodic Celtic music. It was calm for now, but maybe it would grow in vigor throughout the night.

Fox steeled himself as he noticed pack wolves spotting him and murmuring to each other, pointing fingers and gesturing in indignant confusion. More than a few were already approaching the Alphas and asking why he and Star were there. Fox tried to listen in on their answers, specifically Ahren's, but the music, crackling fire, and growing chatter made it difficult.

Star heaved a sigh. Fox glanced at her. Her head was tilted down, her eyebrows drawn together. Fox noticed she was wearing a shirt with a slightly lower-cut collar, which revealed a pair of attractive collarbones, accentuated by a necklace. It was a simple leather band that tied around the base of a single wolf's fang. It had been cleaned and polished, possibly even coated in something that would preserve its integrity. She was messing with it, finger pads rubbing it like one would with a worry stone.

Fox grew curious about it, but thought better than to ask. He didn't know how touchy of a subject it might be with her, especially considering she'd kept it hidden under other shirts she'd worn.

"I think we'll be okay," Fox said, hoping to quell her anxiety as he watched the pack wolves accept whatever explanation the Alphas gave them. They returned to mingling, although they continued to send unhappy looks his way. They hadn't uproared in refusal to their presence, and Fox considered that to be the best he could get.

"I haven't spent time in a gathering like this since I was a teenager," Star admitted. Fox looked at her again. She was still fidgeting with her necklace, and her gaze over the growing crowd seemed both pained and distasteful.

"Were they not good gatherings?" Fox asked. If Star was willing to speak, he was willing to listen.

Star's brows twitched into a frown. "They were when I was a pup. Later on, though, they became dens for bad memories."

Fox had an inkling that Star had grown up in a pack, like most lone wolves did, and something had happened to make the pack dislike her. Or make her dislike the pack.

"Can I ask how?" Fox queried. Star heaved a deep sigh and she adjusted her footing. Her mood seemed to shift from ill nostalgia to justified haughtiness.

"People didn't like who I was becoming. And I didn't care to change for them," she answered. "And pack wolves do what pack wolves do when their fellow members stray from their ways. My parents forced me into therapy like there was something wrong with me. My friends alienated me and started preposterous rumors. Soon my own Alpha had a sit-down with me and told me if I continued down my path, he would have to do what was best for the pack. Some sick boys played cruel tricks on me, and I returned them in kind. Gatherings like this became an opportunity for the pack to humiliate me, or corner me and try to overwhelm me and scare me into changing. Eventually I said, 'fuck this' and I left before they could do anything worse to me."

Fox hadn't quite expected such a thorough response, but it provided the insight he needed into Star's character, to see if she was dangerous underneath her somewhat unthreatening surface. "What were you doing that made everyone dislike you?" he asked.

"Witchcraft," she replied, straight to the point. She looked at him then, her green eyes ablaze with both the firelight and defiance. Her jaw was set, her shoulders pulled back. She was shorter than Fox by half a foot, but he had no doubt she could jump him right there if she felt like it.

Surprisingly, Fox found himself endeared by such confidence. Star was small, but she could hold her own and had the conviction to do it. Fox couldn't help but respect that. Women had it harder than men, out on their own in the wild.

"What deities?" he responded. He wanted to show her that he wasn't perturbed by her practice, even though witches of any kind were always regarded in a bad light. Star's expression grew shocked, caught off guard by his quick acceptance. But then she smiled, a pleased pull at the corner of her mouth.

"Gaia and Artemis," she said. "Goddesses of the earth."

"Your pack didn't approve of your patronage towards them?" Fox asked, confused as to why werewolves would be against following those deities.

"Well, it was more so the origin of the goddesses. If I insisted on witchcraft, they at least wanted me to follow Norse deities. But I found myself drawn to those two. That, stacked on top of me practicing witchcraft in the first place, basically colored me as a deviant in their eyes."

"I see..." Fox murmured. He studied her a little more. She didn't come off as a witch, but that could probably just be a lack of access to materials she needed. She didn't give off any evil vibes, and Fox knew what evil felt like. She was just living her life the way she wanted to.

"Thanks for not recoiling in disgust," she said.

"I'm no saint; I have no right to judge," Fox replied, shrugging his shoulders. She looked at him again.

"Fox, the most docile lone wolf anyone has ever seen, isn't a saint?" she inquired playfully, nudging his arm with her elbow. Fox scoffed lightly.

"Everyone needs to survive somehow. I just try to do it more quietly," he told her.

"Well, I like to do it loudly when the occasion calls," she said. "I tipped Warren off about the town being less full after the storm, and he should have an easier time stealing from a shop. I knew the fucker would get caught. Asshole can't be sneaky to save his life."

Fox raised his eyebrows at her. "You told him to steal?"

Star shrugged and crossed her arms. "Sure did. Now he'll learn to keep his grubby hands to himself."

Her response hinted that Warren had probably tried to touch her in a way she didn't like. Fox had to hand it to her, she was crafty. Her methods of survival seemed to tailor less towards violence and more towards playing people against themselves. His respect for her grew.

The pack wolves had been giving the dining table a wide berth due to their presence behind it, but it seemed their hunger got the better of them, because eventually a few of them came up to get their cuts. After a few braved getting so close to them, the other pack wolves had no problem following suit.

Fox could feel eyes on him as he cut up bits of elk and goose meat, dishing them out onto plates, while Star fulfilled requests for juice or wine. He moved as calmly as he could, trying to portray himself as least threatening as possible. The pack wolves who approached the table came off as tense and cagey, but Fox avoided eye contact and spoke with the best manners he had, and they seemed satisfied.

The night dragged on. The elk slowly withered into bones and fur. The geese became rumpled feathers. The kegs of juice and wine gradually emptied. The pack wolves relaxed after filling their bellies. The bonfire was stoked and fed wood, keeping it ablaze.

Fox watched as the pups who had been brought to the party were shepherded to the spot in front of the hung sheet. An Omega set up torches behind it, and began a shadow play, telling stories of their Celtic origins, and legends of warrior werewolves vanquishing evils, and journeys of long lost mates crossing distant lands to find each other again.

Fox was distracted by such stories for a while, until he noticed the music change in tone. It became more lively, jigs spurring the adult werewolves to dance or sing along. Laughter and wide smiles joined the chatter of the party. Fox found himself overcome with a feeling of sonder; of recognizing that each individual here had a life as deep as his, and he was but a mere outsider, a speck on the edge of their vision.

As he watched the scene before him, his emotions began to rise and tumble together. His heart felt light and full at the sound of the music, but his lungs felt heavy and tight at the feeling of eyes still watching him closely. His skin was warm from the fire and Star's proximity, but his stomach felt cold and empty, not only from lack of food, but lack of nourishment from his own kin. Fox had never attended a party like this, and he wondered how much he missed out on in his youth.

Everyone here was so jovial, even despite the two of them being there. Some pups who weren't interested in the stories were chasing each other on the outskirts of the field, watched by parents and Betas alike. Adolescents clung to their circle of friends and gossiped and attempted to dance. Young adults came back for more and more wine, and soon became the life of the party, cheering on the music and forming an unofficial dance circle in front of the stage. The older adults watched more calmly, talking idly with one another.

Each age group was different, but everyone was together. Everyone basked in this togetherness so easily, so comfortably, so familiarly. Fox's heart surged painfully in jealousy for a moment. Why must he be denied such fun, such festivity, such belonging?

A song ended and another began right away. It only took a few notes to play before Fox found himself jarred with recognition. He knew this song. His mother had taught him the dance to this song, her excuse being that every werewolf should know it, no matter where they hailed from.

Star gasped next to him. "Oh, I haven't heard this song in ages," she said. She looked around for their watchers, but at the time only Ahren was keeping an eye on them.

Star spun around and tugged on his arm. "Come dance with me," she said.

"What?" Fox replied, anxiety filling his veins. "I don't think we're allowed to."

"Look," Star said, sweeping an arm out around them. "The food and drink is all gone. Nearly half the pack is drunk. Everyone is distracted. There's barely anyone watching us. And we've been good this whole time. I think we've earned at least one dance."

Fox's shoulders tensed. He hadn't danced in years, and he didn't know if this would get them in trouble. There were plenty of reasons not to do it. But there was one good reason to do it anyway; to feel like a werewolf, even if it was just for a fleeting moment.

Star let go of his arm, already tired of waiting for his approval. She slipped off her shoes and socks and rolled up her pant legs. She stepped away from the table, just enough to give herself some space to move around without bumping into anything. And she began to dance.

Fox stood there, awestruck and dumbfounded at once, as Star flawlessly followed the steps to the dance, in perfect beat with the music. This song was a long one, but it wasn't too slow or too fast, and it filled the air with nothing but the desire to be free.

The dance began with staying as a human. Star stepped methodically around a wide circle, her arms up and reaching towards the sky, then curling down towards her chest, symbolizing a werewolf's desire to pull the moon and her stars down to their soul on earth. She repeated this gesture, rolling her head left and slowly to the right, face up towards the sky.

Fox glanced around at the pack wolves, but found that no one was paying attention to them. No one except Ahren, and now Evander. Evander had joined Ahren where he stood by the entrance to the bonding sector. Both men had their arms crossed. But whereas Evander was frowning, Ahren was smiling.

Fox swallowed and turned his gaze back to Star. She was still in the beginning of the dance. Fox took in the sight of both the moonlight and firelight on her skin, warm and cool glow mixed together. Her confidence beckoned him to join her. The ache in his chest gave him the last push he needed.

Fox took off his shoes and socks and rolled up his pant legs. He took a steadying breath and pretended that the pack wolves weren't there, that it was just him and Star.

He began to dance. He stepped methodically on the other side of the wide circle Star had been following. His muscles were tense as he raised his arms, his neck not quite wanting him to loll his head to the side. But Star opened her eyes and found he had joined her, and a wide grin broke out across her face as she laughed in delight.

That was enough to make Fox's anxiety fall away. He blushed something furious, though, but he loosened up enough to laugh quietly to himself.

The two of them followed the circle, reaching up towards the sky and beckoning the moon to come down. The dance shifted, and they twirled and mimed claws raking down their own skin, symbolizing the need to shed their human skin and make room for their wolf's fur. This part of the dance, they did just that. Their legs lengthened and morphed into paws, fur sprouting from their knees down to their toes. Their hands grew half lupine, fur sprouting from their elbows to their fingertips, real claws taking the place of nails. Their ears elongated, as did their snouts, and fur dusted their faces.

The song swelled in vigor. They moved together in animalian gestures, feet thumping the earth, claws raking the air, heads miming biting and howling, shaking back and forth as if finally shedding the last of their human nature and accepting the wild beast inside them. They leapt across the grass, backs arching, hands raised to praise the moon, tails swishing back and forth. Something carnal swelled in Fox's chest and he released a yipping howl. Star responded. Fox could hear other pack wolves making the same sounds. Their own howls were lost in their party, so no one noticed.

Fox lost himself in the dance and the music. He and Star leapt and twirled around each other. They circled faster and faster as the song quickened, and as it finally crescendoed, they ended in a pose similar to the start of the dance, hands raised as high as possible, noses to the sky, raised as far up on their toes as they could, yearning for the goddess of the night.

The song ended. Fox and Star panted as they heard the pack wolves cheer and howl in collective joy. Fox checked himself, reminding himself what he was and where he was, and he quickly snapped his arms down and morphed his body to full human again.

Star seemed less concerned. She laughed breathily and receded her fur in far less of a rush than he had. She stumbled forward and grasped his biceps, pressing her forehead to his chest for a brief moment. Fox's breath caught.

"Wow," Star said through another airy laugh. "That was fun."

She pulled herself away and Fox looked over at the Alphas. Evander did not look pleased, but Ahren was still smiling.

"We shouldn't have done that," Fox said. "We weren't supposed to—"

"Fox," Star interrupted. She held her hands out and dropped them to her thighs. "Who cares?"

Fox exhaled a stressed breath. "I just don't want to get into trouble."

"Then why did you dance in the first place?" Star asked accusingly. Fox stared at his toes, half buried in the grass. He didn't answer for a long moment, and Star stepped forward and lightly punched his arm. "You shouldn't be punished for being a werewolf."

Fox swallowed, then sighed. He rubbed his arm where she hit him like it hurt, and she scoffed and hit him harder. "Ow," he said, but she grinned at him. Fox realized she was trying to make him feel better, not worse.

Fox looked over at the male Alphas again. He expected to see Evander storming over, but he just continued to stand next to Ahren like a child would when told 'no'.

The party continued for the next few hours. Soon the older adults left with their pups. Then the teenagers left after their parents. The bonfire slowly died down, and soon the drunk younger adults made spots for themselves in the grass and fell asleep amongst each other. The Omegas went from playing jigs to playing calmer songs, and soon they stopped altogether.

Fox and Star helped the male Alphas and a few Betas kill the fires in the torches and the bonfire. They cleaned up the scraps of food and whatever trash was left lying around, and the Omegas packed up their instruments.

Fox thought that either Ahren or Evander would pull him and Star aside to reprimand them for their violation, but neither did. Evander just looked frustrated, and Ahren looked undisturbed. If anything, he seemed oddly pleased.

Fox found himself yawning before too long. When cleanup was finished, the bunker guard Beta escorted Star back to her bunker, while a tipsy Leyra and sober Sunshine walked with Fox back to their house. Star waved goodbye to him as their paths parted, and Fox waved back with a small smile. He wanted to let her know that her confidence had not gone unappreciated.

At Leyra's house, Sunshine helped her mate upstairs and to their bedroom, while Fox sleepily trailed behind them.

"How did you fare?" Sunshine asked him just as he started to make his way to the spare room. He stopped and turned to face her. She had already placed Leyra in their bed, of which Fox could see over Sunshine's shoulder.

"It wasn't as terrible as I thought it would be," Fox admitted. Sunshine smiled, delighted.

"I'm glad. Good night, Fox," she replied.

"Good night, miss Sunshine," Fox echoed, and she closed their bedroom door as he turned to trudge into his room.

Inside, he tiredly changed into his sleeping outfit and crawled into bed. He groaned softly as the mattress accepted his weight, the pillows fluffy and blankets warm. As he owlishly blinked himself to sleep, a fleeting thought crossed his mind. He had felt alive tonight.

~The song I was listening to when imagining Fox and Star dancing was Would That I by Hozier, if anyone wanted a reference

12, THE OMEGA

Once a month, Fox learned, the Alphas had a meeting at one of their houses. This one was held at Leyra's house.

Fox had just finished brushing his teeth in the bathroom when he heard the voices of the other Alphas downstairs. He poked his head out of the bathroom to get a peek down the stairs, wondering why they were all here. They herded themselves into the kitchen, and as they passed the stairs, Fox could see them carrying paperwork.

Fox went to his room and changed into fresh clothes. After, he made sure to be quiet as he went downstairs. As he peered around the corner into the kitchen, he found everyone making themselves comfortable at the dining table.

He stepped forward just enough to make his presence known, but not enough to invade their space. The Alphas glanced at him.

"Go grab some breakfast, then come back here," Leyra told him.

"Yes ma'am," he replied, and slipped out the back door to make his way across the field.

Breakfast was uneventful. Fox and Star swapped food they didn't like, and no one tried to fight. Afterwards, the lone wolves were sent to spend their day of rest in their bunkers, or within the sector under watchful eyes of the Betas.

Star asked Fox if he wanted to stay there and hang out with her. She could share some of her experiences as a witch and show him what patronage to goddesses was like. But Fox regretfully declined, telling her he still had to serve the Alphas today. Star was disappointed, but understanding, and Fox promised to hang out with her some other time.

He made his way back to Leyra's house. The back door was propped open to let in the cool late summer air. Papers were spread over the dining table, and Sunshine had brought out glasses of iced tea for everyone. The Alphas were engaged in conversation when Fox approached the back door, and he decided to wait for instruction. He settled down onto the back porch steps.

He listened silently as the Alphas discussed various things. Their topics ranged from how the start of the school year was going, to inventory checks of both the farm and medical sectors, to upcoming holiday plans, to going over suggestions made by the pack members.

A few hours went by, and Fox was beginning to think he wasn't needed for anything at all. Leyra had just told him to come back so that he could stay somewhere under watchful eyes, and away from the other loners. It made him wonder if the Alphas purposely wanted to keep him apart from the other lone wolves, either for a reason, or because they had noticed he didn't like them.

Fox felt bad that he had to turn down Star, but maybe it was better to keep his distance from the bunkers. He didn't want to get into a fight with either Seb or Warren.

Fox moved to lie down on his side, boredom causing drowsiness to take over. He'd just begun to doze off when Evander called his name. He jolted and stood up, turning to face the Alpha.

"I want you to run to the sandwich shop in town and grab lunch for us. Take these," Evander said, holding out a couple slips of paper and two $20 bills. Fox reached out and took them. One slip of paper was a permission note, and the other was a list of their orders. "Look at me," Evander said, and Fox met his gaze. "I don't want any pickles or mayonnaise on mine. Absolutely none, understand? If I find either on my sandwich I will make you walk all the way back into town and get a new one."

"Yes sir. No pickles, no mayonnaise," Fox assured him.

"And I want both the exact change and the receipt. If I see that something doesn't add up, I will not hesitate to punish you. This is not your money, understand?" he added, his expression hardening to get his point across. Fox nodded.

"Yes sir, I understand." Evander gestured for Fox to get going. Just as he turned away, Fox heard Sunshine call after him inside the house.

"Oh, Fox! If you'd like, you can take my bike. It has a basket," she said. "It's parked right out front."

"Oh, thank you," Fox replied, surprised that she would let him use her things. Evander narrowed his eyes, but he didn't protest, and so Fox happily trekked around the house to the front, where a sky blue bike was parked by the front door. A sizable basket was attached to the rear, big enough to fit a bag of food with no problem.

Fox hadn't ridden a bike in a while, but bike riding was one of those skills one didn't tend to forget. He mounted the seat and pushed off, gliding down the driveway and turning on the road towards town. As he pedaled, his legs began to feel pleasantly exercised. The breeze swept his hair back from his face, and he briefly closed his eyes as a wave of nostalgia settled on his shoulders. As a pup, he'd ridden his bike almost everywhere.

Fox shook his head and focused on the present. The trip into town was mostly downhill, so Fox happily cruised most of the way. He kept to the side of the road to avoid getting hit by cars, and found his way to the sandwich shop.

He parked the bike in front of the shop, leaning it against a window so he could keep an eye on it while he was inside. He wasn't sure if anyone would try to steal it, and the notion made him nervous. He went inside with the hopes of getting out quickly.

Inside wasn't as busy as Fox had been expecting, much to his relief. But like the visit to the bakery last week, the other occupants of the building began to show their distaste for his presence as his scent filled the space.

Fox tried to ignore the sneers and disapproving frowns from the other customers. He approached the counter, where a young adult manned the register. He grew unsettled by Fox, his shoulders drawing tight and lips pursing.

"I'm here to place an order for the Alphas," Fox explained. He procured the permission note and the paper with all their sandwich requests. The employee's expression relaxed a little as he understood why Fox was there. He took the notes and looked them over. "Can you please make sure there's no pickles or mayonnaise on Alpha Evander's sandwich? He will get very upset if there is."

The employee raised a brow, probably not used to docile behavior from a loner, but he nodded and began making the order. Fox waited patiently, keeping an eye on the bike outside. The sandwiches were finished in just a few minutes, and Fox paid with the money Evander had given him. The employee gave him his change and receipt, which Fox stuffed inside the bag containing the sandwiches, and promptly left.

Fox exhaled soundly as he began riding the bike back to the Alphas' houses. The bag of food rattled in the attached basket, and Fox's stomach growled. He willed himself to ignore it, to not indulge in the food right next to him. He swallowed down the saliva in his mouth and focused on pedaling.

Since the ride back was uphill, it took Fox a bit more effort. At one point he decided to take a break, stopping at the road that led towards the cemetery. He sighed and rested back on the seat, tilting his head up to gaze at the canopy above him.

A few minutes passed of peaceful quiet, where he managed to catch his breath. He had just moved to resume his trip, when he heard a soft moan break through the sound of wind-rustled leaves. Fox paused.

A long moment stretched, and he heard it again. This time the moan held an air of confusion and discomfort. Fox took in his surroundings, carefully scrutinizing anything that moved. Some branches crashed together, leaves ripping, and Fox gasped as his gaze snagged on a boy stumbling out of the woods onto the cemetery road.

The boy fell onto his hands and knees, tripped up by the bushes he'd just walked through, and he whimpered. Fox's instincts flared with a warning, prickling his skin on the back of his neck; something wasn't right.

Fox swung his leg over the bike and leaned it against a nearby tree. He jogged over to the boy, and upon getting closer, he realized it wasn't a pup, but one of the Omegas. Fox stuttered in his jog, unsure of approaching now. Pup or Omega, really, he needed to be careful.

"Hello? Are you alright?" Fox asked, keeping a safe distance. The Omega moaned again, clearly hurt somehow. He swayed on his hands and knees, as if dazed, or so sick he was rendered too weak to get up. Fox sniffed the air, searching for hints of blood or vomit, but he didn't smell either one.

Fox crouched down and tilted his head to get a better look at the Omega's face. His light brown skin carried a faint sheen of sweat. Fox noticed his brown hair was a tangled mess, and his eyes were heavy-lidded, faintly glazed.

What was wrong with this Omega? Had he overworked himself? Had he eaten something that was now causing fatigue? Fox crept closer, just enough to inhale the Omega's scent. Fox recognized an herbal smell mingled with his odor, and Fox wondered if the Omega had accidentally come into contact with a toxic plant.

"Hey..." Fox called, hoping for a response. The Omega blinked sluggishly, then slowly lifted his head to look at Fox. Fox had grown used to seeing how Omegas reacted to spotting him. He expected fear or distrust to fill the Omega's expression, even just a little, but he remained the same. His brows were slightly furrowed, but his eyes didn't seem to register who he was looking at.

"Can you get up?" Fox prompted. The Omega slowly blinked again. His lips were chapped and dry, and he still swayed, just a little.

Fox groaned under his breath. This wasn't good. But there was no one else around to help, and he didn't want to leave the Omega alone to go look for someone. He might get up and wander away, or his health might take a turn for the worse in the time Fox was gone.

"I'm going to lift you onto my back, is that okay?" Fox asked. The Omega's eyes slid closed and his lips pressed tight, but instead of speaking, he only moaned in discomfort again. His arms trembled, threatening to give out, and Fox reached forward and tucked his hands under the Omega's armpits. He carefully lifted him up and shifted him around so he was draped over Fox's back, arms wrapped over his shoulders. Fox held onto his wrists and stood up, and the Omega's feet dangled against his calves.

The Omega whimpered, a soft sound, as Fox began walking. "It's okay," Fox assured him, "I'm going to find you some help."

He paused by the bike and considered his options. He was halfway between town and the Alphas. He had a good chance of finding help back in town, but it was a better idea to alert the Alphas of their Omega's condition right away. Fox wasn't sure what could be in his system, but he didn't smell good at all, and if there was something out there everyone else needed to avoid, the Alphas would need to be the first to know. Not to mention, if he went into town he would be suspected of hurting the Omega himself, which would cause a ruckus he didn't want to deal with. The Alphas knew where he'd been all day, so he should have an easier time explaining himself to them.

Fox looked over the bike, trying to gauge how he would bring it, the food, and the Omega back uphill to Leyra's house. He took a moment to visualize how he would do it, and decided the best option might be to sit the Omega on the bike and keep him balanced while he walked the bike up the road.

It was a struggle, but Fox tried his best to maneuver the Omega off his back and onto the bike. He felt nervous about handling him, moving his legs to mount the bike and placing his hands on his sides and chest to keep him from falling over, but how else was he supposed to do this? He'd have to hope the Omega wouldn't feel violated.

A problem arose when the Omega was fully seated on the bike. He started whining in a wolf-like manner, pained and distraught. Fox looked him over in surprised panic, wondering what was wrong. The Omega attempted to get off the seat, thighs shaking and bare feet scraping the dirt road, his hands pressing down on his crotch region as if to stave off pain. Fox realized that the pressure of the bike seat was hurting his groin, and quickly lifted him off the bike and eased him down onto the ground.

The Omega curled up, hands still pressed on his crotch, but he tried to cover it as well, attempting to shield it. Was he worried Fox would try something, or had someone already done something to him down there?

"I'm not going to hurt you," Fox told him. The Omega's whines died down, but his breaths still came out soft and distressed. Fox weighed his options again. Riding the bike with the Omega on his back would be too difficult and would take forever. He could leave the bike here, but then someone might see it and the bag of food unattended, and help themselves. Fox didn't want to lose Sunshine's bike or the Alphas' food, but this Omega's safety was more important. Surely they would understand.

Fox carefully lifted and maneuvered the Omega onto his back again. This time he made sure to tuck his hands under the Omega's knees and carry him properly, so as to not put too much strain on his arms.

With the Omega securely draped over his back, Fox took off in a jog, as light as he could manage so that he wouldn't jostle the Omega too much.

Fox was used to running with weight on his back. He managed to make it to Leyra's house without issue, and he wasted no time in banging on the front door with urgency. A moment later, Leyra opened it.

Leyra's eyebrows rose in surprise as she took in the sight before her. Fox didn't want to waste anymore time. "Can you help him?" he asked, slightly out of breath.

"Fucking hell, Fox," she swore, and reached her hands out to cup the Omega's face that currently rested on Fox's shoulder.

The tone of Leyra's voice, combined with the scent of a sick Omega, attracted the attention of the other Alphas. Each one crowded in the doorframe to see what was wrong. The Omega caught on to their scents and began whining, but this time it was pleading, not pained, seeking the safety of his Alphas.

Fox crouched down with Leyra and eased the Omega into her arms. Ahren pushed forward and crouched as well, looking the Omega over and sniffing him.

"What the hell are you doing with a sick Omega, Fox?" Evander demanded. Fox swallowed and kept his gaze lowered, staying crouched, hoping that performing submissive body language would keep Evander from getting angry with him.

"I found him on the way back here. He just stumbled out of the woods, all alone. I didn't know what else to do," he explained.

"You did the right thing," Ahren said. Fox lifted his eyes to Ahren's, who held a sincere expression. A bit of relief soothed Fox's nerves. At least one of them was on his side.

"Where did you find him?" Rishima asked, coming around the group to crouch down by the remaining space next to the Omega. She pressed the back of her hand to his forehead, feeling his temperature.

"On the cemetery road," Fox said. "He doesn't seem... responsive. I tried to sit him on Sunshine's bike, but the seat hurt him. I don't know if- if maybe..." he trailed off, not wanting to start throwing out accusations or possible causes of his condition. But Fox could see and feel the Alphas bristle.

Ahren gently brushed the hair from the Omega's face. "I'm going to press on some spots down here, just to see if it hurts. Okay?" he murmured. The Omega just whimpered, still appearing dazed, his eyes sliding in their sockets and his eyelids remaining heavy. Ahren carefully slipped his hand between the Omega's legs and pressed on where his secondary sex orifice would be. Fox could see it was gentle, barely a nudge, but the Omega started whining in pain, like before.

"Sh sh sh," Ahren hushed, immediately taking his hand away and cradling the Omega, who curled up against him. Fox's heart stuttered as he watched a tear roll down the Omega's cheek. "It's okay. We're going to take you to the hospital, alright?"

The Omega whimpered and whined softly into Ahren's shirt. The Alpha stood with the Omega in his arms, and the others followed suit. "We'll take my car," Leyra said, and she went inside to grab the keys.

Fox stood up as well, rubbing his hands down his thighs. Ahren looked at him again. "Thank you for helping him," he said. Fox just swallowed and nodded. "I mean it. You could've left him to protect your own skin, but you didn't. That's something we will always appreciate."

Fox furrowed his brows. He didn't think kindness was a strictly pack wolf trait, but Ahren made it sound like Fox was being very un-loner-like. Maybe he was. Lone wolves prioritized their survival over others, most of the time. Fox looked at the Omega in Ahren's arms, and he remembered that he had once traveled with an Omega, a few years ago. She had been kidnapped from her home pack and had managed to escape her captors. Her journey to find her way back home had somehow involved crossing paths with Fox, who took pity on her situation and wanted to help her. She had told him all about the terrible ways Omegas could be treated, how much like property they could become, and ever since then Fox had developed an underlying sense of protectiveness towards Omegas. He knew pack Omegas were strictly off limits, but he would never pass up helping one.

Fox felt more than a few pairs of eyes on him, and he blinked to find Evander and Rishima staring at him. Their expressions were thoughtful, curious, and Fox's shoulders tensed. "I- I had to leave your food behind. I'll go get it."

"Show me where exactly you found him," Evander said, stepping forward to follow as Fox turned away. Fox nodded and set off walking back down the road. He heard additional feet walking with him, and a glance over his shoulder showed that Rishima was joining them.

Fox led them back to the spot he'd left the bike, then showed them the area he saw the Omega come out of. Evander studied the disrupted foliage and began sniffing the air, catching on to the Omega's scent. He stepped off into the woods, following it. Rishima copied him, and Fox assumed he was expected to come with them. He was curious, too, as to what happened to the Omega.

He trailed behind as the two Alphas tracked the Omega's path through the woods. It wound around a with no clear direction, sometimes circling on itself, until eventually it led to the back gate of the cemetery.

The iron gate hung slightly ajar, barely pushed open. Evander opened it more and stepped into the graveyard. Fox lingered at the gate, uncertain if he was allowed to follow. Sunshine had told him it was a sacred place, and even with Alphas present, he didn't think he was allowed to go in there again.

The Alphas didn't seem to pay him any mind as they went inside. Fox waited, watching. Evander followed the Omega's scent only ten feet in, before he stopped mid stride. He made a sound of disgust, covering his nose and mouth with his hand. Fox couldn't see anything out of the ordinary, though. Rishima came up next to Evander, stopped, and snorted like she had just inhaled something rank and foul.

"Ugh," she gagged and pulled her shirt collar up over her nose. "What the hell?"

Evander turned away and jogged back to the gate. Fox could see his eyes were watery from the sting of the stench. Rishima did the same, coughing and fanning the air in front of her face.

"I'm guessing Benjamin came in here to pay respects and came into contact with whatever that is," Evander suggested. "Smells like some kind of toxic plant."

"Whatever it is, it's definitely coming from inside here. We'll need to let the pack know this area is off limits until we can safely remove the source of this smell," Rishima added.

Fox stepped back as the Alphas exited the graveyard and closed the iron gate. "This doesn't explain his pain, though," Evander noted. He leveled an accusatory look on Fox, and Fox stepped back even more.

"The plant may have made him fatigued, but what made him sore?" Evander questioned rhetorically. "Maybe you thought you could get a quickie in before dragging him to us, giving us puppy eyes and acting innocent while Benjamin was incapable of telling us who hurt him."

Fox didn't like being accused of assaulting the Omega, and his offense made him bold enough to straighten his spine and hold the Alpha's gaze. "I swear, sir, I would never touch your Omegas with ill intent. Omega or not, I would never rape anyone, either," he stated. He felt his chest ignite with justified indignation, a hot anger at being continuously wronged every time he tried to do something right by someone.

Evander's blue eyes locked onto Fox's hazel ones. He searched Fox for hints of lies, for a crack in his nonexistent facade. The intensity had Fox gripping his hands into fists to keep them from trembling and ruining his resolve. He was no monster. He would show Evander that.

A few long tense moments passed. Evander eventually blew out a breath through his nose, nostrils flaring. Fox thought he had accidentally challenged the Alpha, and his heart skipped a fearful beat, but Evander's physique deflated. Fox almost hadn't caught how much the Alpha had puffed up during their stare-down.

Evander pointed a finger at Fox. "One day, lone wolf, I will catch you red handed, and your true self will be revealed."

Fox did his best to take a steadying breath. "I am not a monster."

"Time will tell," the Alpha growled back. Without another word, he turned on his heel and began walking back to the main road. Fox glanced at Rishima, who'd been watching the ordeal silently and thoughtfully. She held his gaze for a moment, her expression portraying nothing helpful, and then she turned to walk after Evander. After a moment, where Fox extinguished the angered flame in his chest, Fox followed.

As the three of them walked back to the main road, he listened to the two debate what kind of plant it could be and why it had started growing in the graveyard. Fox was glad he knew about a potential danger to his health, and he couldn't help but think about Anodyne, who resided not too far away. He hoped he could still visit him without crossing paths with this toxic plant, or with anyone helping to cull it, and he hoped this plant wouldn't affect the naga either.

Fox walked the bike back to Leyra's house. Evander took the bag of sandwiches and counted the change and compared it to the receipt. When he found that everything was accounted for, he then inspected his sandwich for the adjustments he'd asked for. After finding no pickles and no mayonnaise on it, he gave Fox a narrowed-eyed look. Fox stood there, studying him while simultaneously shoving down the need to avoid eye contact. It seemed Evander was secretly pleased, but not happy. He kept waiting for Fox to slip up, and Fox kept proving him wrong.

Fox turned away, but only took a step before he heard Rishima speak. "Here." Fox looked back at her where she stood by the dining table and saw her holding out one of their sandwiches. Probably Ahren's. "For helping the Omega."

Fox glanced at Evander's emotionally-mixed face and tentatively took the sandwich. "Thank you, ma'am," he replied. His stomach groaned and his mouth watered. He stepped out onto the back porch and tucked himself mostly out of sight, where he devoured the food without an Alpha watching.

With the disruption of the sick Omega, the meeting ended early. Evander left after eating his lunch, as did Rishima. Sunshine had left with Leyra when they took the Omega to the hospital, so Fox was left alone in the house.

It felt strange being there, without having snuck in. He felt like he walked on the cusp of trespassing, or like he was a ghost in an unoccupied house. Fox tucked himself away in his room and attempted to nap. But his thoughts kept him awake, of what would become of the Omega, of the toxic plant, of himself in this pack.

Hours passed, the sky outside his window darkened, but he didn't get up to close the curtains. He stared off into space, until he heard the garage door open beneath him. He sat up and listened. He heard the two women exit their car and enter the house. They spoke quietly, enough that Fox couldn't pick out clear words but he could hear the vibrations of their voices. They moved into the kitchen, and Fox got out of bed.

He left his room and went downstairs. In the kitchen, Sunshine heated up a late dinner in the microwave.

Leyra spotted him as she poured herself some water. "Benjamin is okay," she stated, and a tight ball in Fox's gut unraveled. He hadn't realized how inwardly worried he'd been for the Omega. "There were traces of Angel's Trumpet in his system, which caused his fatigue and confusion." Fox frowned at this, as Angel's Trumpet didn't tend to smell foul. "As for his other symptom..." she glanced at Sunshine, whose expression twisted into disgust and anger, and Fox didn't like seeing such a dark expression on Sunshine's normally radiant face. "Someone did rape him, but dna test results didn't come up with anyone specific. Whoever did this to him had kept anonymity in mind."

Fox's gut clenched in discomfort. He couldn't imagine how violated Benjamin must feel. "What about scent?" he asked.

"Couldn't pick one up. He just smelled like plants. And you, but we know you didn't do this," Leyra responded. Fox exhaled and frowned. At the thought of plants, he wondered if somehow the tropical plants in the conservatory had managed to spread into the area outside, but he didn't know if those plants could survive in this climate. Maybe all the thunderstorms had made it possible. He couldn't help but tease the notion that maybe something had happened inside the conservatory itself. He would have to ask Anodyne if he had seen anything.

"Well... I'm glad he's okay," Fox said. Leyra nodded in agreement.

"Lucky you found him. I'm happy that you helped him, instead of taking advantage of his vulnerability," she said. Fox felt a sting in his chest, a residual hot flame from earlier in the day, but smaller and less likely to ignite. Sometimes he really hated being a lone wolf, hated constantly being lumped in with horrible werewolves who succumbed to dark desires. Lone wolves like him were few and far between, he knew, but they weren't nonexistent.

"I really hope I don't come off as someone who would do anything vile like that," he murmured sullenly. His gaze had trailed down to his feet, his shoulders slumping and head tilted down. He heard the soft padding of bare feet on the kitchen floor, and then a pair of hands were taking hold of his shoulders and straightening them back up. Fox flinched and found himself staring at Sunshine, who stared back with an immovable resolve.

"You don't," she said, firm and true. Fox's eyebrows drew together in uncertainty. Sunshine's hands squeezed his shoulders. "You don't," she repeated. Fox swallowed and looked down again.

"Are you hungry? Come have some lasagna," she said, and patted one shoulder as she turned to retrieve their dinner from the microwave.